THE WEIGHT OF RAIN

A Collection of Short Fiction

T. C. EMERYS

April Showers Publishing 2020

Dedicated to Celia and Ray, my wonderful parents.

CONTENTS

Furious teal waves flood in.
I'm sinking.

SUNFLOWER

SUNFLOWER

Everything inside me glows red, but the people who pass me on the street see nothing.

My pain is invisible to them.

It is hard to describe to someone who doesn't have chronic pain what it feels like. Everyone has known physical pain, whether it's a broken arm, childbirth or just a stubbed toe.

But when its chronic, you view pain in a completely different way, and people view you in a completely different way.

"I'm sorry," I say, eyes closed as I wait for his voice to slap me with his disappointment. The phone rests on my ear as I lay on my side, wrapped in a blanket.

His silence, even for the briefest moment, is just as heavy as the words I'm dreading from him. The tension has been there for a while.

"I know, but..." he says, words pregnant with the sentiment he hasn't yet expressed. I think he will today. I don't want him to.

"I'm sorry," I say again, as if the repetition will make him understand.

"Eira, you've just given me this excuse so many times."

There it is. He's brought out the elephant in the room, trumpeting and swinging its trunk furiously.

"Sunny," I start, although I don't have anything to finish with. I know he has more to say, and in spite of my hurt, I know I have to let him get it out.

"What are my parents going to think?" he says. There's some bitterness at the end of his tongue, I can hear it even through the phone, punching every consonant so that it subtly lashes at me. He answers his own question before I can interject, "They're going to think you don't want to spend time with them."

"Can't you just explain that I'm not well?" I say. It sounds reasonable in my head, but I know that every other person hears a faint echo of *faker* in the background of my words. They read between lines that aren't there.

"No," he says, "You know I can't. No one is ill this often."

No one is ill this often.

And that's the truth for the majority of the population. Everyone has little aches and pains, winter colds, hangovers. But living in true pain, day after day? That's not plausible in the minds of the average person. If they can't imagine it happening to them, how can they empathise?

Before I was diagnosed, the doctors used to ask me to put my pain on a scale. They used numbers, as if pain can be quantified.

Counted. Added. Divided.

Subtracted.

"Ten," I would say confidently, and even the doctors would raise their eyebrows a fraction as if to say *A ten every day? That's just not realistic.*

I didn't like the numbers. Numbers didn't say what I needed them to.

I liked to think of my pain in colours.

Blue for that dull ache that sits in my gut for hours at a time.

Bright opalescent pink for the fizzing feeling of a flare-up just starting.

Fuming red and all-encompassing black for the top tier of only-swearing-will-cover-it pain.

Cloying grey for that cloud that rolls over the mind after pain has taken over. Brain fog. Rowing a boat out onto open water in dusky light and not finding your way back.

"Eira?" Sunny's voice interrupts my chain of thought. I realise I've been silent for a while.

"Can't you just try to explain?" I say, "I really can't face it."

I know that my euphemistic language isn't helping me, but I feel the need to soften it for him. We haven't been dating long, I don't want him thinking of me in pyjamas I haven't washed for days, alternating between curling up against a blanket and living in the bathroom.

"Can't you just take your medicine? You told me you had medicine for your... condition."

I want to correct him and say "conditions", but I know that wouldn't mean anything to him. The way he pauses before saying the word "condition" stabs me hard, but I fight back the stinging feeling of frustrated tears in my eyes and say quietly, "It doesn't really work like that."

He doesn't say anything, and I hear him give a slight sigh, so I add, "I really want to be there."

"Then be there!" he says, exasperated, "I'll look after you."

"I can't," I sit up a little, as if the added uprightness will lend my voice the conviction that he's unable to hear, "This flare-up isn't going away."

"Flare-up," he repeats, not mockingly, but almost as if the

word doesn't have any meaning to him, as if there's a hollow space between us where my explanation should be.

I think about giving more explicit details, but I can't bear to.

"Tell your brother I wish him a happy birthday, and please apologise to your parents," I say, "I'll meet them soon, I promise."

"Mmhm," he replies, little empathy left in his tone.

"I'll speak to you tomorrow," I say. I wait for him to say "feel better soon" or something that might release the knot of worry that is forming in me, but he doesn't, so I just add in desperation, "Miss you."

"I've got to go - Mum's here to pick me up."

My heart thuds emptily as I swallow down something angry at how dismissive he sounds and just say: "Okay."

He's already hung up.

"Those are the same tracksuit bottoms you've had on for the past two weeks," Mum says as I enter the kitchen, a blanket pulled around my shoulders.

She tuts as she grabs a tuft of my hair, the curls knotting around each other.

I don't say anything, just walk to the sink and pour myself a glass of water and start to head back upstairs.

"Excuse me," Mum says, and I turn slowly to look at her, "Have you eaten today?" she asks, but it feels like an accusation.

"No," I say, pulling the blanket tighter around me, "I don't feel well."

"I know," she says, "But you have to eat something. You'll feel better with some soup inside you."

There's no use arguing; she's already started opening a tin of mushroom soup.

"Mum, I can't eat that – it has wheat in it," I say. She came to all of my doctor's appointments. Gastroenterology appointments. Dietitian appointments. But she either ignores it or forgets.

"Oh," she says, staring at the open tin, "Never mind, I'll have that. What would you like?"

I know there's no use telling her I'm not hungry, so I think of the only thing I can bear to even consider eating and tell her: "A Yorkshire pudding."

Mum knows this is one of my go-to foods when I'm ill, so she doesn't question the strangeness of eating a plain Yorkshire pudding, just pulls the gluten free flour from the cupboard and starts making it.

"Thanks Mum," I say quietly, before heading back upstairs.

She knocks on my bedroom door some time later. I've dozed off without even noticing, hood up around my face, curled on one corner of the bed. There's rain hammering against my window. It's relentless but comforting.

She opens the door a crack and purses her lips as she sees me.

"You really should try to get up and do something today," she says, judgement starting to creep into her tone. She holds out the plate, three homemade Yorkshire puddings sitting in the middle of mashed potato and gravy. I take the plate and take a Yorkshire pudding from the top, still not able to face the gravy or mash just yet.

"I'm not feeling up to it," I say.

"You had an argument with Sunny, didn't you?" she says. I furrow my eyebrows at first, unsure of how she would know that, but then I realise she must have been listening to my phone call.

"Yes," I reply simply, chomping on the crispy edge of the pudding.

"What happened?" she says, sitting on the edge of my bed.

"He wanted me to go to his brother's birthday party tonight," I reply, waiting for the lecture to start.

"To meet his family? How exciting!" she sighs, "Why did you argue about that?"

"Because I'm not well enough to go," I mutter.

"Oh silly, you'll be fine," she says, "You're just nervous."

I don't reply. There's nothing to say to that. She knows about my conditions. She sees my pain.

The silence changes the tone and she looks away before standing up, "If you're sure," she says, "Nan's coming over tonight – maybe have a shower before she does?"

I don't reply again, taking another bite of the pudding.

"She'll want to see you. Make sure you come downstairs for a bit?"

"Thank you for the food," I murmur, trying a spoonful of mashed potato.

"No problem," she says, lips still thin with disapproval as she leaves the room, pulling the door to.

"You're looking so slim!" my nan says brightly as I try not to fall down the stairs. I'm dizzy from my medication and my stomach is still sore.

"Hi Nan," I say, kissing her on the cheek, "Lovely to see you."

"You have lost a good few inches," she says as she hugs my

midriff gently. I breathe her in; her fabric softener reminds me of Dad - her son - the warm white smell of him, wrapping me up in nostalgia for a moment.

I try to ignore the comment about my weight, but as we lean back from the embrace she's looking at me expectantly.

To her, it's a compliment. She's saying I was overweight before and now I "look better". She doesn't understand that how I look and how well I am are often at odds. I've only lost that extra stone or two I wasn't supposed to have because I can barely eat anything without pain coursing through me.

I'm the least healthy I've ever been, despite my BMI being in the "good" range.

There aren't any words to explain all of that to her. It's not that she doesn't care, she just wouldn't understand it. It's an alien world to her. I just smile and say, "Thank you."

She drops it, satisfied with my reply.

"Where's your boyfriend?" she asks, "I was hoping to meet him at last."

"They're not speaking," Mum chimes in with an accusatory look at me and a raised eyebrow at Nan to indicate she shouldn't talk about it.

"Oh," Nan says, squeezing my hand and smiling, "Don't worry, plenty more fish in the sea."

"Margaret," Mum says in a warning tone before adding, "Let's eat some dinner. Are you going to join us Eira?"

"Yes," I say, anxiety gripping me. My head knows I shouldn't be forcing anything down right now, but I can't bear to say anything in front of my Nan.

Mum dishes up chicken, boiled potatoes and vegetables and the three of us sit at the small kitchen table. I pick at the potatoes and have one or two pieces of carrot, but I can't bear to eat anything else.

Nan doesn't seem to notice, she's enjoying chatting to us.

"When Wyn was small," she says, the mention of my

father's name sending invisible shockwaves through both my mum and I. It's been a few years since he passed away, but his name still has that affect on us. "He used to hate peas," she continues, gesturing to her plate, "And one day, I moved the cabinet we had next to the kitchen table and found loads of peas crammed down there."

"Eurgh," I say, wondering why I've never heard this story before.

That's something I've noticed since I lost my dad. I thought I knew him inside and out. What he liked and disliked. And yet, the more time that passes since he died, the more stories I hear about him that I'd never heard before.

"They were all dried up, must have been there for ages," Nan says, "I asked him about it, and he said 'Mummy, I don't like peas', so I never gave them to him again."

"Sounds like Wyn," my mum replies. My Nan's stories can be long and rambling, but we treasure them – any extra snippet of Dad, however dull, brings a little part of him to life, just for a moment.

Dinner flies by with reminiscences: summer holidays spent at Barry Island, Dad spending hours on sandcastles and refusing to go in the sea.

Nan glows when she speaks about him. I sometimes forget that she was his mother. I sometimes forget how she must feel now that her only child is gone.

"Promise me you'll come to the club soon," Nan says, hugging me tightly as we see her out of the door.

"I'll try," I say. The club is a green bowls club and it's Nan's second home. After Grandad died, she sank into the welcoming arms of the people there. For her, the actual sport of green bowls is secondary to that beautiful feeling of community that she's discovered there. It's something I yearn for in my own life.

Among the older men and women who make up the most

part of the club, my Nan has found herself friends, grief support and an endless number of people who enjoy her loquaciousness.

"We're having a social night on Friday - how about that?" Nan says, one foot out of the door, cane supporting her as she leans back into the doorway to ask.

Her eyes are pleading with me; this is important to her.

"Go on," Mum whispers.

Fear grips me, the same way it does whenever I'm pushed to make plans. It's the fear of knowing that every day, every hour even, is a dice roll. I can't guarantee whether I'll roll a double six or snake eyes.

"Okay," I say, deciding to take the unfavourable odds, and I'm immediately glad I did as a huge smile bursts across her face.

"Wonderful," she says, "You can meet all of my friends! Wear comfortable clothes, nothing flashy."

Perfect, I think. Even if I'm having a flare-up, I'll get away with wearing tracksuit bottoms.

"I don't think she owns anything other than comfortable clothing Margaret," Mum teases.

I'm thankful to find myself feeling better than usual on Friday – I was dreading having to cancel on Nan, having to ring her and hear her obvious disappointment.

It is quite obvious when I walk in, arm in arm with Nan who is not that steady on her feet these days, that Tintern Green Bowls Club doesn't have many twenty-year olds among their members.

"Meg!" a woman near to the door says, coming and taking my nan's other arm. I've never heard anyone call my nan anything other than Margaret before.

"Hi Hazel," Nan replies, kissing her friend on the cheek, "This is my granddaughter - Eira."

"Oh, my goodness," Hazel replies, swinging round to look at me, "Wyn's daughter?"

"That's right," Nan replies proudly.

Several other women have overheard who I am and come over, greeting me warmly, their friendliness overlapping into a round of words and sentiments. Evidently, most of them knew Dad and I'm grinning hard enough to make my cheeks sore listening to them remember him fondly.

They usher me to a table laden with papers. It's quiz night, and the ladies are excited to have someone younger on the team who can, in their words, "answer all the Tok Tok questions". I somehow doubt that the grey-haired man who is leaning against a microphone at the other end of the club-house will have included any Tik Tok questions, but I enjoy feeling useful and wanted.

The first round is a picture round, mostly daytime TV personalities and politicians, of which I know very few.

"That's Bruno Tonioli," one lady, Joy, says very confidently, but as this is one of the few faces I actually do recognise, I quietly correctly her with:

"That's Gino D'Acampo."

My contribution, however, is drowned out completely by the sheer noise of the other people at the table.

After a few rounds of questions, a lot of which I'm pleased to find that I know, the quiz master sets up a quick-fire session, handing out tiny bells for each team to ring to 'buzz' in our answer.

"You're the youngest," Nan says with a grin, "So you'll be the fastest person to ring. Ring it even if you don't know the answer. One of us will I'm sure."

My task is clear and I smile a beaming half-moon, and a river of adrenalin flows into my arms as I ready my hands.

"In what year," the elderly quiz master starts, reading each word slowly so that my fingers start to itch against the stem of the bell, "was Queen Elizabeth II's coronation?"

Ring!

My bell and another one, two tables away ring at almost the same time.

"Table two," the quiz master says, and I groan as I notice our brass table number screwed to the wooden centrepiece – the number four - shining mockingly.

"1952," I look to get a glance of my bester and notice the speaker is also in his twenties. He, like me, looks marvellously out of place here, and yet he's smirking with genuine enjoyment too.

He has short mousy brown hair, spirals that hold their shape around his head and light brown skin.

He notices me looking and flashes me a smile. I don't quite manage a smile back before he's turned away again.

"Correct," the quiz master says, continuing even slower than before, "Question number... two... Which English city houses the Bodleian library?"

Ring!

My hands are shaking with the excitement – my bell got in before his.

"Table four," the quiz master says, and I breathe with relief.

I hear the ladies start to whisper to me, but I already know the answer, "Oxford," I say clearly, and as I watch the quiz master nod, I see in my peripheral vision the young man turn his head to look at me as I speak. I don't look at him this time, I don't want to look like I'm gloating. I force myself to stare straight forward at my Nan and her friends, feeling his gaze at the edge of my eyeline.

"Well done," the quiz master says to me, "Question three..." he takes a sip of his water and splutters slightly as it goes down the wrong way, "Question... three..." he says again, hacking in between words. I wonder if he's okay, but he's recovered before I can voice my concern to the table, "Who voiced Woody in Disney Pixar's anima-"

Ring!

We're both in before the question has finished, and a couple of the other tables are chuckling at our keenness. I glance over at my competitor with red in my cheeks and he's looking back at me.

"Yes..." the quiz master starts, and coughs again before he can say a table number.

Neither of us wait for permission: "Tom Hanks!"

We've both shouted the name simultaneously and the lounge room is filled with tittering laughter and people talking under their breaths as we wait for the quiz master who has pulled a hanky from his pocket to cough into it.

After a few moments he pockets the hanky saying, "You can both have the point."

I ready a smile for my opponent, but he's leaning into his table, talking with his teammates so I turn back to my own table to a firm pat on the back by Joy and a hand squeeze from my Nan.

The night ends with a hand of cards to settle a tie between the top two teams, although our team was nowhere near the top. His team, however, was. He plays 21s against a man in his sixties from another team, who despite the casual attire of most of the attendees, is buttoned up in a waistcoat and tie.

The younger man doesn't win, but he shakes hands with his challenger and politely sits through a half-serious lecture from one of his teammates about experience before youth.

I hang around chatting to Nan, orange juice in my hand, waiting to see if he will be left alone. What would I say to him if I went over?

A pithy one-liner about pipping him to the post?

A simple hello?

But an older man comes over, says something to him and he nods and stands up, following the older man behind the bar where he picks up a black half-apron and ties it around his middle.

After a few more words exchanged with the man, he heads through the cellar door behind the bar.

"Home time, Eira," Nan says, yawning, "It's nearly my bedtime I think."

"Stay for another vodka and tonic?" Joy says to my Nan, "I'm buying."

"No, no, Eira should get back, and besides – I'm driving!" she laughs, and Joy pulls down her lips and chortles. "Iechyd da!" Nan says before swigging the dregs of her drink.

"Sorry, of course you are," Joy laughs, kissing Nan on the cheek as we start to head out.

I follow her out of the lounge, one eye on the cellar door.

I'm thankful Nan wanted to leave – I'm exhausted and my medication will be wearing off soon, but I can't help but feel a pang of regret that I hadn't been bold enough to speak to the young man after the quiz. A previous version of me – a pre-diagnosis me – wasn't the shy type. She would have spoken to him. Befriended him. Gained that feeling of community that I'm so desperately missing now.

We drive back in comfortable silence, both tired from our evening out.

"We had a lovely evening," Nan says at my door, a little tipsiness on the edge of her voice as she speaks and I'm worried Mum will notice, "Thank you for coming, Eira."

"Thank you for having me," I say, hugging her tightly.

"My grandparents asked where you were," Sunny says. He's on fire with the embarrassment of my absence the week before. I had waited for him to call me, after a few very terse texts the night of his brother's birthday party, but it has taken him all this time to reach out.

He's still angry, and I can't help but feel he has a right to be. Mum has spent the week telling me what a shame it is I didn't go, and using my evening out with Nan as an example of 'what happens when I go out and socialise'. No matter how many times I tried to tell her I was having a good pain day the night of the quiz, she waves a dismissive hand and tells me I owe Sunny an apology.

"Mm," I say. I'm disappointed that I sound squeaky and scared. I want to be firm and brave but I'm second-guessing myself.

"Grandma made her saag paneer especially for you because I told her how you cooked it for me once."

"That was kind of her," I say, "Please tell her thank you."

"No," Sunny says firmly, "You should have been there to say thank you. It was the fourth time that I've had to make an excuse for you. My cousins were teasing me saying that you don't exist."

"Sunny..." I say, pulling myself up to say something, to be clear with him about my illness, about how it affects my life.

"I told them you had food poisoning – again! They didn't believe me," he sighs, and I can sense the conversation unravelling around me. He's not going to listen even if I can be brave. Even if I voiced it perfectly, chose every word to make beautiful phrases, even that wouldn't be enough.

"You shouldn't have lied about that," I say quietly.

"And what should I have done?" Sunny mutters, "I can't do this anymore."

I knew it was coming, but the shock that falls from my

lungs down to my pelvis is paralysing. He doesn't say anything more.

"Okay," I say, but it's not.

My mind spirals with all the ways I'm not worthy of his love.

I want to scream that I'll try harder to be at family events, but the untruth won't leave my lips.

I'm already trying so hard to pretend to be a different kind of well that I'm breaking. I'm at my limit.

"Okay?" he spits back, "So, we're done?"

"I don't know what to say," I reply truthfully, but the truth isn't what he wants. He wants illusion. The illusion of wellness.

"Fine. We're over. Have a shitty life," he says, and the phone cuts off.

Researchers say that you can't remember physical pain. Of course, you can remember how awful it is, enough that you want to avoid it. That's just natural instinct, but the actual feeling of physical pain is illusive.

It's like a song you knew long ago, and you can remember the title and the artist, but for the life of you the melody alludes you.

And it means that you can't fully prepare for physical pain, because no matter how long it's been since you last experienced it – seconds, days, weeks – it's return is still in some ways a shock. The absence of pain isn't something we notice unless we train ourselves to, and because of that we don't know when to feel happy that our head isn't aching or that we don't have back pain.

Because of this, its return becomes an "oh yeah, that's

what that's like" moment that takes your breath away and chips away at your hope.

That's just one of the ways that pain is intricately cruel.

I think about that as I lay against the pillow of my bed, my tears soaking into the pillowcase turning the light blue into a stormier grey. This is one of the rare moments in my life that I am in intense emotional pain, but no physical pain.

Sunny's final words to me sting. They were childish, and I try to convince myself that he didn't mean it, but I think deep down he did.

He saw into my soul in those childish and mean-spirited words. He saw the future relationships I would have that would be sapped of something by my pain. He saw my work life, tainted by days off and unproductivity. He saw my future children, unborn and unable to understand why.

That's what the darkness tells me as I lean into the pool of my own tears. It's the same darkness that threatens to pull me under when I'm trying to deal with physical pain.

The same darkness that tells me there's no hope.

It's a liar.

My phone flashes in front of me: *Ivanka E. wants to send you a project!*

It's a notification from SelfEmployMe.com, an app I use for work.

At eighteen when I left sixth form, I knew I would never work a 9 to 5, as much as Mum wanted me to. Dad passed away when I was fifteen, and he'd always hoped I'd follow in his footsteps to become a lawyer.

After he died, it became increasingly obvious that Mum had always hoped that too.

After a few teenage years kidding myself that I could be an academic, a quick-mouthed litigator like Dad, I realised that I didn't want it. My body didn't want it, but neither did my heart. The thing about other people's hopes is that they're not relevant to you. And that's hard to accept when you want to please the people that you love.

Luckily for me, I had other talents.

When you spend months, cumulatively years, of your life bedridden, you learn to find other things to do.

For me, it was video editing. I never wanted to be a YouTuber, a smug millionaire at the end of a selfie-stick telling you about their daily life, but I do love taking clips and turning them into videos.

"Hi, Ivanka," I start typing, "How can I help?"

She replies immediately, "I need a video edited for Tuesday. It is a YouTube commercial for my company. Can you do the job?"

"Absolutely," I type back, "Let me have a look at the clips you sent over."

It started as a hobby, clipping together mobile phone recordings of the pet dog on Windows MovieMaker, but Dad got me the proper software for my fifteenth birthday. With the help of a family friend who worked as a freelance journalist, I made a portfolio of example videos on my YouTube channel and signed up to websites to find clients.

When you have no idea what level of pain you will be in from one moment to the next, a job with some flexibility in it is key.

The message pulls me back from my reverie and I get to work, spending a few hours discussing the project, arranging payment and organising the video clips.

After a few hours of work, my phone buzzes again – Facebook Messenger.

Sunny, 6.03pm
Can we talk?

I want to fire back something hurtful. To make him feel how he made me feel, but I know I'm done with him.

I open my phone and write back:

Eira, 6.04pm

About what?

Sunny, 6.04pm

What do you mean? We can't leave it like that.

Eira, 6.04pm

You broke up with me.

Sunny, 6.04pm

Yeah, I did, but surely you want to stay friends? Or are you that cold?

Eira, 6.05pm

No, I just don't think it's a good idea.

There's a delay where I can see the blue dots moving along the screen. He's thinking hard about his response and I don't know what I'm hoping for.

Do I want to be his friend after the things he said? No. But I could never stand confrontation. I don't want him to be angry at me.

Sunny, 6.06pm

Fine.

The message is short. I wonder what he typed in the first iteration that was so long.

Then the blue dots start again.

Sunny, 6.07pm
> *You're fucked up anyway.*
> *Don't message me again.*

I want to feel shocked or surprised, but I actually feel relief. He's shown me who he is over the past couple of days.

I feel calmer now.

I click the info button in the top right corner and sigh out my tension as I click the 'block' button decisively.

I lean back against the headboard of my bed.

My eyes are dry.

My phone vibrates in my hand and I look down, a small pang of fear that I hadn't properly blocked Sunny, but it's a text from Nan.

Nanny Bryth, 6.10pm
> *Social night again Friday. Curry night! Shall I tell Janet in the kitchen about your food thingies?*

Nan has never really understood my conditions, but I'm pleased she's thought about me.

Fear grips me at the thought of explaining my dietary requirements to the volunteer cooks at the club – one wrong move, accidental or not, and I'd be suffering the consequences for weeks.

But I really want to go. I had such a good time at the quiz.

I think about what to reply and then type:

Eira, 6.11pm
Sounds great – don't worry, I'll bring food for me.

That's the easiest solution. Sure, I might get some stares as I pull my Tupperware containers out, but it's better than risking it.

Nanny Bryth, 6.14pm
That's probably for the best luv. Can't wait to see you, kiss kiss.

The club members queue up eagerly at the buffet style table that's set out at the opposite end of the lounge to the bar. Janet's proudly serving up her concoction – I can see the empty jars of Patak's and plastic packaging of pre-cooked Tandoori-style chicken from Costco through the server's hatch of the kitchenette area, but it smells incredible and she's neatly lined up garlic naans and poppadoms on a separate table.

Meanwhile, I'm sat at a table with Nan, two Tupperware containers in front of me, one filled with overcooked white rice, the only kind I can stomach, and the other with a fragrant but lukewarm serving of homemade paneer curry *sans* chilis, onion, garlic, or any other foods that are on the "banned" list for my conditions.

I feel a little awkward as the others start to sit down at the table with their plates, their eyes looking from the containers to me and back again, but Nan is by my side. She's waiting to get hers until I've started eating, and I can feel her protectively hovering over me.

"Go on," she says gently, telling me to start as the two other people that have joined us dig into theirs, "I'll be back in a second."

She heads toward Janet, and I gingerly pick up my travel cutlery and put some curry onto my spoon.

"Fancy seeing you here."

Someone sits down in the seat Nan has just vacated and it takes me a moment to clock who it is. I have my head dipped down to take in the spoonful of food. I look back up to see the young man, half-apron round his waist.

"Oh, hi," I struggle to reply through my spoonful, covering my mouth with my hand so that he doesn't see the food whirling around like a concrete-mixer.

"Hi," he says, a smirk on his face as he realises he caught me off guard.

"Nice to see you again," I say as he starts tucking into his own meal.

Nan returns with her plate and raises her eyebrows as she notices the young man in her seat. I shrug and she smiles, sitting down at a different table.

"Oh sorry," he says, half-standing to offer the seat, but she waves a hand at him and tells him to stay where he is. "Your grandmother?" he asks me.

"Yes," I say.

"I'm Malachi," he says, "I work behind the bar," he continues, gesturing to the apron, "My dad runs the bar," he points to the older man I saw him with last time, currently eating his curry perched on a stool behind the bar.

"He lets you fraternize with the members then?" I ask playfully. I'm please that I'm managing to shed some of my shyness.

"Yeah. It's a really quiet bar. The members like a drink, but they're hardly doing Jaegar bombs. Dad lets me join in on social nights so long as I clean the pipes the next morning so he can have a lie-in."

"Sounds like a fair deal," I say, "And I suppose free booze whenever you want it?" I add sarcastically.

"Oh absolutely, I can pound back a litre of sherry on an average shift," he says matching my tone. "That leads me swiftly into asking if you'd like a drink – on me, of course," he adds.

I'm tripped up by this – I wasn't expecting the offer.

"Oh, um, yes... please, an orange juice please," I say.

"Really?" He says with a small chortle, "You know we've got beer, vodka, the works – I'm paying so you might as well fleece me while you can."

"Oh, I can't drink alcohol," I say, cheeks glowing pink as I try to think how to explain, "I, uh..."

"Say no more, orange juice it is," he says, putting me back at ease as he stands up to head over to the bar, "If you're lucky, I'll give you a cocktail umbrella."

"Thank you," I say as he walks back to the bar.

I continue eating and am quickly interrupted again.

"You're Meg – uh, I mean, Margaret's – granddaughter, Eira, is that right?" One of the other ladies at the table seems to have noticed I'm alone.

"That's right," I reply, smiling politely.

"Are you at university?" the lady to her right asks, and they both watch me intently. I see Malachi out of the corner of my eye returning with a bottle of orange juice, a pink cocktail umbrella and paper straw poking out of the glass neck.

I'm surprised that I feel embarrassed to answer "No."

"Oh, so you've graduated, or..." the first woman presses as Malachi sits down and slides my juice across to me. I smile and mouth a thank you as I think about my reply.

"No, I, uh," I start.

"You didn't go?" The second woman chimes in.

"That's right," I reply quietly.

"Me neither," Malachi declares, ripping a naan bread in half, "It wasn't for me."

I'm washed with relief as I see he's noticed my embarrassment and is offering a helping hand.

"So, what do you do, Eira?" The first woman says, still staring at me with an almost unnerving intensity.

When people ask, 'what do you do?' they mean 'how do you earn money?'

And what they really mean, whether consciously or not, is 'what are you worth to society?'

Fifty years ago, when these ladies were around my age, the answers around a similar table of people would have been quite straight forward, and thus the summation of an entire person by their profession far more easy to judge: 'lawyer', 'bar staff', 'journalist', 'doctor'.

"I'm a freelance video editor," I reply, noting the immediate looks of confusion on their faces.

They can't pin that down, they're wondering 'what does that actually mean?' and 'is that highly paid?'

Sometimes I want to scream when I'm asked this, despite the other person's good intentions.

Not all of us have the luxury of a 'standard' job. A nine to five. A 30k salary and a private pension.

It's not their fault – they're not meaning to be tactless, they don't understand that what I want to answer is that 'what I do' is survive.

I eat.

I sleep.

I work when I can.

That's what I do.

That's all anyone can do.

"Is that something you're passionate about?" Malachi asks. I'm both surprised and elated by the question as I can answer it confidently.

"Yes," I reply, a smile creeping back onto my face. "It is."

"That's wonderful," he replies.

"Do you work for the BBC?" the second lady asks, still not clear on my answer.

"No, I'm freelance," I reply, "I mostly work for Youtube artists or make web advertisements."

"But not the BBC?" she adds again.

"No," I say, noting the look of disappointment on her face. I'm presuming the next remark she had ready was about the BBC and I've scuppered her plans.

"And does that pay well?" the first lady asks.

I can't think of how to answer and just stare blankly back at her.

For a start, I'm not sure what she considers 'being paid well', but I'm struck by shame as I consider my earnings.

I know I'm a low earner – the HMRC remind me of that every time I do my tax return. I pay Mum a small rent and I probably won't be able to afford my own place.

"Well, this place pays peanuts," Malachi says with only a hint of irony. He looks to the side to give me a smile and I can tell he's used to dealing with these people. This is his social area of expertise. He has a confidence that I envy.

"Tsk, you'll have to ask your Dad about a raise then

Malachi," the second lady laughs heartily.

"I'm sure he'd give you one if you closed up every now and then," the first lady asks.

"Very funny," Malachi says, joining in as the two ladies laugh at their own remarks, "I close up all the time, I'll have you know!"

They continue back and forth, and I take the opportunity to finish my food.

Malachi is so at ease in the way he speaks to them – I can imagine him behind the bar, holding his own.

I wonder if I could have ever had a public-facing job like that.

I've always been shy, but even more so since my diagnosis ten years ago. Socialising got harder. Days, weeks and sometimes more were written off when I was ill or struggling with pain.

It quickly affected my way of speaking, and I noticed it with Sunny especially. He dominated the conversations and when he would push for a reply, I would give a non-committal response or say what he wanted me to.

As the night draws to a close the two ladies move to another table to talk to friends, leaving me and Malachi by ourselves.

The ladies have monopolised the chat, and whilst I've tried to chip in, I've been happy to let Malachi take the lead. They seem to have their own sociolect here, a way of speaking that only they know. A type of humour and social code that takes time to learn. As I rightly assessed, Malachi is an expert.

"Are you free tomorrow?" Malachi asks, placing his knife and fork onto his plate and standing up, ready to take it back to the kitchen.

"Um," I start, weighing up the risk of each answer. On the one hand, committing to another outing would be doubling the chance of a flare-up, but on the other hand, turning it down when I am currently feeling well seems over-cautious.

If do too much in a short space of time, even if I don't have a flare-up, I could suffer the consequences in the days following. This is an idea explained by Spoon Theory. The idea is that your energy is contained in finite measures – "spoons" – and that you only get a certain number of "spoons" each day.

If you burn through your spoons one day, you may find yourself with less spoons the next day.

I have to plan my rests, because if I don't, my body will do it for me.

"Nothing too exciting," he assures, perhaps seeing the look of indecision on my face, "I'm going strawberry picking with Dad. Just thought it might be fun if you tagged along," he says, and his relaxed tone does put me at ease. There's no pressure or expectations.

"Strawberry picking?" I say, not sure what that entails.

"Yeah, there's a pick your own farm in Fordbridge, a ten-minute drive from here. You pick whatever fruit you like and pay for what you've picked at the end. It's good fun."

"Ah, I live in Brockweir and I don't drive," I say, heart racing.

"That's okay, I'll pick you up if you like?"

He's putting everything in place to make this happen. I feel grateful for his kind offer, but worry still swims through my mind.

I pause for a moment and he looks at me with a mixture of hope and worry. He doesn't know why I'm thinking about saying no, but he can tell I'm hesitating.

"Okay," I say, "Sounds great."

"Ah, that's brilliant," he says, "It'll be fun, I promise. Here, let me write down my number, text me your address?"

"I will."

"Grab that one," Malachi says playfully, "Oh, and don't miss that one."

He's teasing me – I've picked almost every ripe strawberry I've seen, carefully piling them into the punnets.

Malachi's dad is ahead of us, occasionally turning back to give a knowing smile as we joke around.

"Stop it," I say, matching his tone.

I'm having a lot of fun. Malachi is easy to be around and he hasn't made anything difficult for me.

When I asked if we could stop and rest, he didn't bat an eyelid. He didn't give me a pitying look. He just sat with me.

"Are you sure you've got all of the strawberries you wanted?" he says with a chuckle, gesturing to my three overflowing punnets, one of which has a broken handle from where I've overloaded it. "Here, let me take one."

He takes the broken punnet, supporting it with one arm around it and a hand firmly under its bottom.

"Thanks," I say, "I think I went a bit overboard."

"I think you did," he nods with a widening smile, "Let's take them to get weighed and put them in the car? There's loads of other things to see here."

Turns out I bought seven quid's worth of strawberries, which made Malachi's dad, Clément, belly laugh and pat my arm.

We load them into the car and Clément heads to the small café on site for a coffee while Malachi and I wander back out into the farm.

The strawberry field is clearly the big draw; it's rolling expanse of green leaves and black tarpaulin is full of families and groups harvesting the berries. The view is interspersed with signs and prompts for the tills and café.

The rest of the farm is wide open, with a field of sunflowers, some apple trees which aren't bearing fruit yet, and a penned off area full of goats.

We amble up the centre of the farm. Malachi's talkative and flies through stories of his childhood.

"Mum went in 2014," he says, nodding sadly as he finishes telling me about a holiday they had taken the year before.

"I'm sorry," I say, my voice quieter than I intended. I want to tell him I lost my dad, but I don't want to insert myself into his moment.

I breathe out, a blue feeling of unsaid words hovering over my chest.

"Thanks," he says, "She was ill for a long time."

"Cancer?" I say and immediately regret it as his face flashes with micro-expressions of grief.

"Yeah," he says, "Colon cancer. She had colitis, diagnosed as a teen."

My heart races at the mention of colitis – a chronic bowel condition. Just like mine.

"I'm so sorry," I say, and I blink to fight back the red-hot tears forming at the edges of my eyes.

I can tell that he's noticed that I've been affected by the conversation, but where words had flowed so easily moments before, now he's doesn't seem sure of what to say.

I look at him a couple of times, building myself up and finally say: "I lost my dad."

"Oh, Eira, I'm sorry I didn't realise."

I can see his own pain being pushed backwards as he empathises with me, and I feel guilty for bringing up dad.

I feel his fingers brush against mine as we walk, and as I look down, he entwines his with mine. Warm orange spreads up my arm in surprise as the weight of his hand swings with mine.

I can't help but smile at him, and he smiles back.

Sometimes I have to remind myself of these moments –

the absence of pain, the feeling of joy. You have to teach yourself to focus on the blank spaces of your body before and after the pain, just so you can bathe in that feeling. It's that hope that will get you through the next flare-up.

Because sometimes the flare-ups are right around the corner.

We walk further, still smiling, still orange with happiness.

Then -

Red.

Stunning red.

Speechless red.

Spreading up through me as we head past the field of sunflowers.

I try not to stop walking, but it grows, becoming an insistent tremor along my left side.

Malachi notices. Perhaps I gripped his hand too tightly involuntarily.

I don't look at him, but I can tell there's confusion, worry, questions.

I can't speak for fear of crumbling. I just keep putting my feet down, hoping he won't say anything. Hoping that I don't have to stop.

We make it to the end of the field of sunflowers before I'm overtaken. I stop and grab his forearm unconsciously.

He can see the pain in my face now and his worry pours from him, purple waves crashing over my head, drowning me.

"Are you okay?" he asks finally, watching me, attentive.

I try to smile, try to be dismissive of it, but I know I'm not convincing, "I'm fine," I say, my voice punctuated by the gruff pain.

"No, you're not," he says, and despite myself I feel a pang of insult. I don't want him to save me.

"I'll be okay in a second," I reply, but my shoulders are

hunching against the stabbing in my gut now and I can feel his disbelief.

"I should call an ambulance," he says, taking out his phone. He makes it to the second 9 before I can reply.

"No, no ambulance, it's not serious," I say. Of course, I don't mean that − I just don't have the words right now. It is serious. What I mean to tell him is that's not urgent. It's everyday stuff. It's my normal.

"It looks serious," he says, gently supporting my arm with his as I start to double over more, "Let's sit," he adds, looking around for a bench and realising there are none. Although the sky is clear, it's rained recently and so he takes off his jacket and puts it down on the wet grass. We sit down, Malachi allowing me to lean into him as I crouch and then sit.

Sitting is worse. The crumpling of my muscles and fat presses against the rogue point in my gut. I lay back instead, my plait pushing into the dewy grass.

The sky is blindingly blue and its beauty teams up with the relief from the pain, the knot that had formed loosening as I lay flat.

Malachi lays back with me and as I turn my face to meet his eyes, I see the spark of recognition. I wonder if he remembers similar moments with his mother.

He doesn't say anything, but I can feel the pressure lift from both of us as he understands what my life is like and he accepts it.

"Are you hungry?" he asks after a few minutes of just laying, looking at the sky.

I check in with myself. Now the pain has stopped, I notice I'm ravenous.

I sigh deeply, allowing the fresh green of the grass against my bare neck to rush through me.

There's that beautiful absence.

"I could eat a strawberry or two."

PARSNIPS

PARSNIPS

There's a silent rule in British families, even ours, that you don't argue on Christmas Day.

We're surrounded by the people we love the most, incredible food, more nostalgia than we can swallow down and yet it is still a Herculean task not to rip each other apart.

I don't think I've ever enjoyed a Christmas Day. Even as a child it was a messy affair. Being the eldest of three - and with twelve years between me and my youngest sibling - made Christmas a chore. I don't remember a time that it was just me, although I know the three years before Tab was born must have been heaven for my mum.

Mum likes to say she "took a break'" before having Ace nine years after Tab, but it was an unspoken fact that Ace, although beloved, was not intentional. Although, it was a source of contention whether any of us were intentional.

No one in our family uses their given name. I was born Genevieve, but Bowie's *Jean Genie* hit the UK charts in the winter of my last year at primary school, sparking a torrent of not-so-inventive nicknames, and I have gone by Ginger ever since. It was an easy switch – I inherited Mum's auburn bird's nest, ghostly white complexion and freckled face. Whoever my dad was had barely made a dent in my genetics. We almost looked like sisters in the '70s, especially as she was only sixteen when she had me. Two red-headed, bony, unruly girls, the disgrace of our small Gloucestershire village. Their disdain only fuelled our rebellion, and we took glee in their blushes.

My sister Tab, formerly Tabitha, shortened her name to the monosyllable at university where she proudly studied Politics, with more of an interest in punk music. To say Tab is beautiful is an understatement, and I, with my matted ginger brush of hair and five-foot-nothing stature have always looked wistfully at my younger sister. Tall, dark brown skin, curls that she styled gracefully, unlike me, and a gentle way of speaking I had always lacked. In our teenage years, extended members of the family had labelled me "gobby" in the way older people do, whereas Tab was "sweet" and "well-spoken".

Our youngest sister, Ace — Candace, briefly known as "Candy" during a phase with leg warmers and pigtails - was similarly gifted in the looks department: golden skin to my anaemic look, Mum's freckles, but with shiny brown hair that she kept just shorter than her ears.

Ace is the kind of person who wants to change the world by doing absolutely nothing. She's absorbed all of Tab's fire and none of the action. She bangs on about the climate crisis with a stainless-steel bottle strapped to her hip, but her house is always full of half-drunk single use water bottles. She lectures us about carbon emissions whilst refusing to use the bus. She describes herself as a philanthropist because she donates a couple of quid a year to a snow leopard.

That's not to say she doesn't have her good points. Ace was always the best one at handling Mum. As the baby of the family, with nine years between her and Tab, and twelve between her and me, she was able to form a completely different relationship with our mother, who by that time, to quote Mum herself, had "gotten her shit together", by which she meant she had found a steady job and had more than two coppers to rub together. Ace grew up with more money than the rest of us, and while we resented her for it, we agreed it made a world of difference to Mum's temperament. She loved Ace, possibly more than she ever did the rest of us.

Of course, Ace grew up to be more of a problem than a joy for Mum, constantly looking for handouts to "find herself" in any country with a hot climate and locals who would happily only speak in English to her. Mum, being an old-school hippie, was only too happy to oblige.

"None of my other children have such a free spirit," she would say as she signed the cheques, Ace snatching them up without so much as a "thank you".

Growing up, we all knew that we looked different to one another. At some point, Mum must have said that we had different dads, although I don't remember when. We didn't press her on it, and she didn't say much further. If I'm honest, I'm not sure Mum knows who our dads are.

We've never cared to know. We've never needed anyone else. We have Mum.

Now, it's Christmas Day 2019 and Ace is being just as selfish as always. We're feeling festive and we bite our tongues.

"This is Robbie," Ace says. She's let herself in with her key, the rest of us gathered in the living room watching the clock on the mantelpiece keep count of each hour over her expected arrival time.

"Robbie?" Mum says, staring at the quiet, considerably younger man on Ace's arm. No one says anything, we're all just staring. He's handsome, a gym sort of person, just Ace's type. His braids are tied back tightly, smoothing any hint of a wrinkle in the creases of his eyes, but even so he can't be more than thirty-something.

His age isn't what's bothering us – it's his presence at all. Christmas Day has an unspoken rule – family only. And a month of dating does not qualify someone to be part of our family. She knows this. There's glee in her smirk.

I'm aware I may sound bitter. Do I resent my sister? Perhaps a little. But we have always been united in one thing: disdain for our grandmother. There's nothing like mutual loathing to bring two sisters together.

"Robbie?" Gran, now ninety-three, pipes up. She's barely said a word to us over the past decade and we presumed she was either going deaf or was so uninterested by her grandchildren's lives that she chose not to pass comment. "Marigold, speak to your daughter."

Ace tries to shoot me a look, but I'm in agreement with Gran for a change. Our usual shared bond is laying like a broken cord in front of us.

Gran used to be our main source of strife. When I was small, she refused to come to Christmas Day. Mum had gotten a council flat a month or two after I was born, in part to seek independence and in part to get away from Gran's conservatism. On that day, Gran declared her cut off. Growing up, I used to think of my Gran as a cartoon villain, a Disney stepmother, self-serving and punishing my mother. It wasn't until Ace was born that Gran came back into our lives, and as I built a relationship with her throughout my teens, I realised that she wasn't the evil witch my imagination and my mother's immaturity had made her out to be. Her only daughter had gotten pregnant at sixteen, just a year after she had lost my grandfather. I'm sure you can imagine a conservative village in Gloucestershire in the 1960s had their own thoughts to add, and Gran was pushed out of her clubs and friendship groups. Whilst her prejudice against single-motherhood mustn't be excused, it took me until I was sixteen myself to realise that Gran was desperately lonely, and any cruelty she had shown my mother and I was her way of expressing it.

I can't say she has ever been a particularly kind person; her stoic upbringing combined with her staunch conservative views have made her somewhat cold, especially when placed next to Mum's sunny liberalism. Christmas Day in our teenage years would often end with arguments, Mum screaming through tears that she wished "Dad was the one who was still alive" and my Gran bellowing back that this is "not how one behaves at the dinner table". Ace's presence at these meals eased some of the tension as the years went by. As she grew up and she was able to converse with the adults, she was easily able to appease Gran, who took a shine to her sanctimonious self-presentation. She defaulted to mothering her whenever she was on the outs with her actual daughter. If only she knew how Ace really felt about her.

Now, crippled by emphysema from years of social smoking, Gran is far mellower; she still holds the same opinions, she just doesn't have the energy or the wherewithal to express them anymore.

Mum is now seventy-five, an age none of us thought she would ever reach given her clumsiness, fondness for Schnapps, and her frankly alarming ignorance of the Highway Code. But here she was, still cooking a mammoth dinner for us every year.

I arrived that morning, bottle of red wine in hand (which was immediately snatched up by the host with a wink and a "good girl").

"Merry Christmas," I said, dropping my coat over Gran's armchair, eliciting an upturned eyebrow from her.

"Drink, Ginger?" Mum called, already opening the wine I had brought.

"No, thank you, Mum," I replied.

I crouched by Gran's chair and looked into her face until she noticed me. A small smile appeared, and I kissed her on the cheek before saying, "Merry Christmas!"

"Oh!" she said, "Yes, Merry Christmas."

The doorbell rang, and I headed to open it. It was Tab and her husband Will. We embraced in turn, relief washing over me as my allies entered the fray. Will was a carbon-copy of Tab. He had slightly better taste in music, but the same militant political views, and even loved the same foods as her. As such, we were natural friends, just like Tab and I, and the three of us were the only family members who regularly congregated willingly.

"No Ellie?" I asked hugging my sister.

"She's with Daniel this year. She's far too cool to hang with her mum anymore. Plus, he has the new baby and she wanted to spend Christmas with her new stepbrother, I suppose," Tab replied.

"A shame not to see her, but honestly a new baby might be preferable to our day," I murmured, taking her coat and hanging it on the banister, "Good to see you, Will," I added.

"Ace's already here then?" Tab asked. She knows me too well. Whilst Tab has never had quite the tumultuous relation-ship with our sister as I have, she understands my pain. None of us make a habit of visiting her; a phone call a few times a year is good enough.

"She hasn't graced us with her presence quite yet," I said, taking the bags of presents they had brought through into the living room.

Tab greeted Gran, who was already dozing off and we left her to it, heading to the kitchen to find Mum finishing the cooking.

"Where is Ace?" Mum asked, hugging Tab, "I thought she was coming with you?"

"Straight to Ace, Mum really?" Tab said, only half-teasing.

"Sorry dear, I'm just worried about her, it's not like her to be late," Mum mused, stirring some congealed bread sauce.

Tab and I met eyes in recognition of Mum cherry-picking Ace's personality. Ace is a habitually late person. We have often joked that it is a skill of hers to be hours late to anything she is invited to. Tab and Will's anniversary the previous July started at 4pm – Ace rolled in, already drunk, at nearly 10pm.

"I'm sure she'll be here soon, Mum," I said through clenched teeth. I fired off a question mark-filled text to Ace in a futile attempt to prompt her hasty entrance.

After a few more hours of small talk and drink, we finally sat down in the living room with a box of Quality Streets, letting our chewing fill the awkward silence of Ace's absence.

We all instinctively turned as we heard Ace's key turn, but none of us were prepared for the two sets of feet that entered.

At last, after the awkward introductions and Gran's outburst, no one quite knows what to say.

"Marigold, speak to your daughter!" Gran says again. Gran, too, has broken an unspoken rule – there's to be no upset at Christmas. Mum doesn't say anything, and Ace, seeing she's gotten away with her unexpected guest, continues with a quick chortle:

"How is everyone's Christmas going?"

"Mm," comes the very British reply, no one wanting to commit too much enthusiasm to the day's events.

Ace plonks herself on the sofa next to the Christmas tree, piling roughly wrapped presents under its boughs.

"Robbie is a male model," Ace starts telling us as she hangs a stocking up on the mantelpiece. We decided this year to do Secret Santa stockings, although as she's the last one to put it up and in plain sight, I can see she got me. My name sparkles in garish glitter glue on a stocking I presume she made herself, given the state of it.

Everyone's staring at the stocking as Ace continues spouting about Robbie.

The gaudy green letters read 'Genevieve'.

It's a slight. A small one, but it must have been conscious. No one in the family has called me by my full name in years, not even Gran. It seems to be an inside joke between Ace and herself because the corner of her mouth is curled upwards again in fiendish delight.

"Oh, a male model," Mum nods, half-listening, her eyes on the stocking too. She flits them over to me for a moment, but my face is as blank as I can make it.

"Yes, I've just started modelling swimwear," Robbie says, and we all turn to look at him now. His voice isn't what we expected from his wide frame – it's timid and polite, and for a moment I feel deep sympathy for him. Clearly he isn't comfortable with being dragged to our family Christmas either.

"Swimwear?" Mum says with confusion, "It's December!"

"Yes – they shoot all of the summer items the previous winter and the other way around with the winter clothes. We flew to Egypt for the swimwear – it's far warmer there at the moment than here."

"I can imagine," Mum says. I can see she's interested, but she's still struggling to make small talk with the unexpected guest.

"Robbie loves travelling too, Mum," Ace adds with a flushed smile.

"How on earth do you shoot the winter clothes with the nice snowy backgrounds?" Mum says, barely noticing what Ace is saying.

"Iceland, in the Spring," Robbie says quietly, and we all nod our heads and 'ah' as if we already knew that.

"Is dinner ready?" Ace says, "I'm Hank Marvin."

"It's been ready for hours," I say under my breath.

"Yes, good idea," Mum says cheerily, "Let's head to the conservatory?"

We all head through apart from Gran, who is more comfortable in the living room with a tray on her lap. I give her a kiss on the cheek as we head through, which is rewarded with a tut. Gran isn't one for displays of affection. I think about asking her if she's okay by herself, but I don't. It seems a silly question to ask her. She's always been an island, even when surrounded by the entire family.

An eight-seater dining table is crammed into the tiny conservatory so that we have to push our bums up against the sideboards to get through. Getting out is more of a struggle than getting in with our expanded waistlines and Brussel sprout bloat.

"I'll bring the dishes through, Mum," Tab says, watching Mum start to panic in the kitchen as various items go back on the heat.

"I've got the sprouts and gravy," I say, sticking the gravy in the microwave for a few seconds in an attempt to loosen the congealed ooze it's turned into while we were waiting for Ace.

I head through with the now boiling hot jug of gravy and the still cold sprouts and put them in the centre of the table. Ace and Robbie are sat hand in hand on the other side and Will is trying to make polite conversation with them about his plumbing business.

"Oh god, the parsnips!" I hear Mum shout and I head back to the kitchen to find her pulling them out of the grill in a waft of smoke.

Tab fans the smoke alarm as Mum places the ceramic dish on the hob defeatedly.

"We can salvage them, don't worry Mum," I say, taking a

pair of tongs and digging through the blackened ones on top to try to find some that are still edible.

"They're ruined," Mum says on the edge of tears.

"No one will miss the parsnips," Tab says, "They're just an extra, not the main event. Look at the turkey – cooked to perfection!"

"Gran loves parsnips," Mum says, "She'll be livid."

"She won't notice," Tab says confidently, putting a lid on the parsnips and putting them back in the now empty grill.

"I'm spitting feathers in here!" Gran shouts from the other room, giving all three of us a jolt as we wonder whether she heard us.

"I'll take her a cuppa," Tab says quietly, putting the kettle on.

"Slip some brandy in it," Mum says sarcastically, "Then maybe she won't notice the missing parsnips.

Within the hour we're sat down enjoying our meal, Slade and Wings blaring out in the background.

"Cracker?" Mum says to Ace on her left-hand side, offering the end.

We brace ourselves for the pop as we each offer our crackers to each other, the small rush breaking the awkwardness for a moment and the table is filled with laughter and discussion over whose hat is whose and whether anyone wants a plastic ring with a huge flower on it or a spinning top.

Then we fall to quiet again, everyone preferring to eat than talk. We feel censored with a stranger in the room, as if he's here to judge our family and how it functions.

I think about how strange we must seem to him. I wonder what his family is like and why he's not with them on Christmas Day. Perhaps we seem idyllic to him if his own family didn't want him round.

"Great turkey, Mum," Ace says, spooning a few tablespoons of cranberry sauce onto the edge of her plate. I furrow my eyebrows as one, two, three, four spoonfuls hit her plate. She notices and looks back at me in challenge, "Do you want some?" she asks.

"No, thanks," I say, rolling my eyes, "Not that there's any left if I did."

"I can scrape it off my plate and onto yours," she says, not taking her eyes off of me. She's calling me out, a small action that usually wouldn't have been noticeable if it wasn't for the silence around the table.

"No, thank you," I insist, returning her gaze. A second passes, and we both break the stare, going back to our food.

"What did everyone get for Christmas?" Mum says, trying her best to raise the tone of the conversation. I notice she's thumbing the end of her fork nervously and I realise how hard today has been on her.

Her energetic question is met with little enthusiasm from any of us.

Robbie isn't solely to blame for the atmosphere this year – there's an absence in the room that he's not responsible for: Ellie. With her at her dad's this year, the average age of our Christmas group has skyrocketed, and any sense of wonder or excitement has plummeted.

Tab was the only one of the three of us to have a child. I expect Mum always thought I would be the one to give her grandchildren as from a young age I dreamed of having a family of my own, much to Tab's scorn. My biology had other plans for me. I will never be a mother in the way I wanted to be.

Ellie has always been our only spark of youth, someone to hold up the mirage of Christmas all on her own. Every present she opened, every mouthful of mince pie, every belted out carol, our younger selves experienced it along with her, remembering the joy of our own childhood Christmases.

I'm not sure what age she stopped maintaining the dream

for us, maybe ten, maybe older, but we selfishly mined her for every drop of joy that we could, until we finally relented and realised she was a teenager.

"Did Robbie get you something nice?" Tab says, a little too prickly.

Ace's eyebrows fold. I guess that means he didn't get her anything she would like to mention.

"Will gave me this ring," Tab says with a smile, trying to bring up the mood, "For our five-year anniversary."

"Oh lovely," Mum says, reaching over and taking Tab's left hand to see the ring.

"Well done, Will," I say with a wink at him.

"If I'd have known we were having crackers, I wouldn't have bothered," Will says back to me, holding up the flower ring that had fallen out of Mum's cracker.

Everyone chuckles, apart from Robbie who looks down wistfully. I'm not sure what his facial expression is. It seems to be embarrassment. He's the outsider here.

"Let's see if you last longer than your previous marriage," Ace says under her breath. It's uncharacteristically forthright, but the bitterness that seeps through the insult is all natural.

That was why Ace didn't answer Tab. She's jealous.

"Um, Ace, sweetie," Mum says quietly.

"Did you really just say that?" Tab says to Ace slowly, looking to Mum for reassurance. Mum is usually the positive one, especially when it comes to Ace, but even she doesn't look like she can understand the comment. Tab is chuckling, but I think it's incredulous rather than amused.

"Oh, come on," Ace says, swigging her wine defensively, "It was a joke, don't be so sensitive, Tab."

"I don't think talking about my divorce is very funny," Tab says sternly.

It was tense before, but now the switch has been flicked.

We've crossed over from light-hearted passive aggressive jabs to actual insults.

I'd hate to be in Ace's shoes – Tab is not someone to be trifled with.

"Well, I do," Ace says with an over the top chuckle, "The irony of your wedding vows. You were so insistent that you had to be married, that you'd last forever."

"If you remember, Daniel cheated on me," Tab spits back at her. I notice she's gripping her fork, which has a potato speared on it, probably unconsciously, but I gently place my hand over hers anyway.

"I do remember," Ace says, "I also remember you spending a lot of time with Will before you were divorced."

"Don't you dare," Will says.

"I'm sorry Will, this isn't really about you," Ace says.

"You're insulting my wife!"

"Marigold, where are the parsnips?" We hear from the other room.

No one replies.

"Don't bother," Tab says gently to Will, "She's never had a relationship that's lasted more than a few months."

"That's true," Will agrees, going back to eating his dinner.

Mum's silent. She's precisely slicing layers off of one of her Brussel sprouts.

"What Robbie and I have transcends time," Ace says on the edge of tears, and I see Tab roll her eyes, "We feel like we've known each other all our lives."

It's laughable. I have second-hand embarrassment. It's not the speed with which the relationship has moved – that's quite usual for Ace – it's that she's emulating her teenage self. I haven't missed that side of her. I wonder if it ever really went away.

As we sit with the ridiculous romantic comment, none of us are taking it very seriously.

It's Christmas.

We're unusually merry, with the wine flowing, good food and the promise of a new year just around the corner, all serving to diffuse the bitterness flying across the table. We're glowing, somewhat drunkenly, but we're in the mood to forgive.

Robbie looks mortified by the conversation, awkwardly shuffling back in his seat.

There's a gap – a moment where Ace should be apologising to Tab for what she said. She doesn't, but it's implied. We all accept it. She's family.

But she's not finished yet.

Robbie gets up from the table suddenly. We all watch him leave, including Ace. I can see on her face that she doesn't have a clue where he's going either.

We all listen for the creak of the stairs to see if he's going to the bathroom, but it doesn't come.

Ace rushes out after him and we hear hushed arguing in the hallway.

A few minutes later the front door slams.

Ace comes back alone.

"Are you okay?" I ask.

"He's gone home," Ace says, face unusually pale.

"Sorry, Ace," Tab says.

"He's coming back," Ace says petulantly, but she doesn't believe her own lie.

"Come on, Ace," Tab prompts. Despite her quick temper, she's the peacekeeper of the family.

"Don't act like you care about me and Robbie," Ace quips.

"I'm allowed to care, I'm your sister," Tab replies, the calm tone she's chosen coming across as supercilious.

"HALF-sister," Ace spits back with more venom than any of us had expected. I watch Mum's face carefully.

"Don't act as if you two don't feel the same about me," Ace says to us and we have nothing to reply.

We're sisters – that was unspoken. We never questioned that.

Mum looks crushed. Our different parentage has been something behind our family history for so long. It wasn't an issue. None of us ever made it an issue.

In Mum's face I can see the shame she feels, undeservedly or not, mingled with the love she feels for all of us and the anger that's building at Ace's disrespect. Anger isn't an emotion she wears often. It colours her cheeks like rouge and narrows her eyes into gaping sores.

She's mortified.

"Don't, Ace," Tab warns, and I see Will grab her hand under the table.

"Enough." Mum whispers.

Ace is looking at Mum now too. She realises what she's said can't be taken back. I don't think Mum has ever spoken to her in this tone before, low and hurt.

Even so, she continues casually, brushing off our pain like we're strangers.

"Why did no one make parsnips... where...?" Gran says from the living room. She sounds distressed now, and I use the opportunity to leave the conversation in the dining room.

I slowly pad through the kitchen and to Gran, who is still sat in her chair.

"Are you enjoying your Christmas dinner?" I ask, bending down so that my eyes are level with Gran's.

"Parsnips..." she says gently and my heart bounces down through my stomach as I hear her slur the 's'.

Gravy is sliding down her knee as her left hand limply holds the edge of her dinner tray.

The left side of her face is drooping, her lips quivering as she tries to speak to me.

"Mum!" I shout as loudly as I can, before turning back to Gran.

I'm struggling with what to say to her.

"It's okay Gran," is all I can manage. I want to comfort her, but fear has hold of me.

"Pars..." Gran says again, and tears form in the corners of my eyes.

I hear Mum heading through the kitchen towards me as I pull my phone from my pocket and dial for an ambulance.

"Oh god," Mum says, rushing to Gran's side just as Gran's grip on the plate gives up and she drops it to the floor.

Mum holds her hand, calmly reassuring Gran. I wish I could be like her – be able to dig deeper into myself to be selfless.

I rest my head on Mum's shoulder as I speak to the operator.

"Ciggie?" Ace says as I join her on the rain-drenched patio.

"God, yes," I say, taking one and balancing it between my lips as Ace lights it.

Gran's in the hospital. As suspected, she had a stroke, not her first, which made it all the more terrifying for Mum.

The cold, battle-ready woman of my childhood is currently laying in a hospital bed, assaulted by drips and breathing tubes.

The doctors say she will recover – she's strong and responding well to the treatment.

Besides, we know she's far too obstinate to die on Christmas Day. She would hate the fuss. Decorations swapped for mourning wreaths. How uncivilised, she would say.

"How was she?" Ace says, the cloud of smoke leaving her lips being cut into tiny pieces by the driving rain.

"Poorly," I say, although I'm aware as I say it that the word doesn't do the day justice. She nearly slipped away from us.

"Poor Gran," Ace said. There's no affection in her voice, merely pity, possibly the most insulting emotion to offer Gran. She would hate the idea of being thought of as ill or frail.

"Yes, and poor Mum," I say. We both know that I don't just mean because of what happened to Gran.

Ace's words – calling us 'half-sisters', especially – will have a lasting effect on Mum. I wonder if it's a bridge that will ever be crossed again. Or would it be better just to forget it?

"Poor Mum..." Ace murmurs. She's being careful of her tone, I can tell. It doesn't come naturally for her to think before she speaks. Her eyes stare forward, unfocussed and thinking and I can only imagine she's playing the scene out in the air in front of her, the memory of Christmas dinner floating in the rain.

"So, Robbie..." I start, trying to think of a way to broach the subject now that everything has calmed down.

She almost chuckles, her eyes refocussing with a blink and turning towards me, "Yes, Robbie," she says with a roll of her eyes.

I'm not sure if its regret that flits across her face or merely embarrassment but she waits for me to say something. To approve or disapprove.

"He seems nice," I say slowly.

I picture the face he made when Ace came out with her mushy comments. I wonder why he agreed to come here – it seems as though he hadn't thought about Ace's family as real people.

"He's a romantic," Ace says, confirming what I was thinking. He romanticised it all. Her. Us. Christmas Day. That's why he agreed to come. He was sucked into Ace's rose-tinted world view for just long enough to dismiss his evident doubts.

"Yes," I say, "But... are you actually together anymore?"

"No," Ace admits, "I don't think so. Not after today. I'm not sure what went wrong."

"Well," I say, a little humour peppered into my tone to try and keep it light, "You could have just *not* brought him round in the first place."

"True," she laughs, "That was... wishful."

"That describes you in a nutshell."

"Wishful?"

"Dreamy," I clarify, "You've always been dreamy."

"I suppose so," she says, "That's why I need you."

"What do you mean?" I scrape my now dying cigarette against the brick of the back wall.

She's never said anything like this to me before. We operate solely on aloof interactions and light-hearted mutual mockery.

We've never waded into the depths of each other.

"My older sister," Ace says with a final puff that fills the space between us so that I can't see her face for a moment.

"Less of the old," I say.

"I mean it," she replies, "I need you, even if I do spend a lot time pushing you away."

I don't know what to say.

I push her away too, but neither of us has ever admitted it before.

I open my mouth to reply, but all that comes out is a half-sigh. I shake my head and lock eyes with her.

"I'm you," Ace says, flicking her cigarette into a bucket by the backdoor, "Just twelve years younger."

ALL CHANGE PLEASE

ALL CHANGE PLEASE

What thought was in your mind when you left?

You'd stayed home from work that day. You were feeling unwell, you said. You wanted to rest to be ready for your big presentation the next day. You were splayed out on the sofa as I left, one hand on your balls, the other on the remote.

Was it a split-second decision? Did you run upstairs and pack without a second thought? Had you planned it for years?

Did you feed the cat before you left? Did you ring your mother so she wouldn't worry?

Aye, you hung up the wash, but that was all. Two sodding tea towels and your gym shorts.

I came home to find them soaked through from the rain. I had to put them in the dryer.

Did you plan it to the hour? Or did you hold your breath as you walked out, bargaining with fate to keep the neighbours in their houses? The last thing you would have wanted was a conversation with Annette from two doors down.

Did you know it was going to rain? I saw you took my red umbrella.

There you were, duffel bag in hand, the one I bought you for Christmas last year, just a few pairs of boxers and your toothbrush inside. All you could grab while the house was empty. You didn't know how much time you would have. You must have thought about taking the laptop. Or your father's RAF uniform.

But you didn't know what time the kids would get home. You didn't know what time I would get back from my hospital appointment. You couldn't risk me coming home to find you packing.

What would you have done if I had left early? If I'd arrived home, come into the bedroom, finding you filling a suitcase with your possessions? Would you have lied to me? Would you have been able to look me right in the eyes and tell me a lie?

A train. Any train. You knew you couldn't take the car. It's far easier to track you that way. Number plate identification and CCTV. A train was the answer. The police showed me CCTV of you disappearing as you boarded a train at Glasgow station, impossible to locate on the carriage as a sea of commuters milled around you, your unknowing accomplices.

They checked every video. Every stop between here and Dundee.

Where were you going?

They think you got off at Gleneagles. They're guessing. The guard checked everyone's tickets after that, they said. He didn't recognise you when they showed him a photo. The one from our wedding day. You, in a bowtie. Me, smiling.

I've combed through the house so many times looking for what could be missing. Did you take a lunchbox or did one of the kids leave it at school?

A sock goes missing in the wash and I wonder if you took it to mess with me. When will I stop taking a mental inventory of our life together?

When will the monotony end? Sleep. Work. Repeat.

Your children miss you. They don't miss me.

Your betrayal has made you even more precious to them. Your absence has made them love you more.

Did you know that would happen? Did you want that? Will you contact them one day?

Will they be thrilled to have you back? Will they be bored of me – the one who stayed?

How far from home are you now? The police say there was only one other train at Gleneagles when they think you got off, although they can't see you boarding it. It was a Caledonian Sleeper on its way to London.

Was someone waiting for you in England? What could they offer you that I couldn't?

A life without children? Without responsibility?

A life without me.

What thought was in your mind when you left? Did it burn you, make you feel guilty, accuse you from the inside out? Was the thought of a new life waiting for you too good to resist? An irresistible person out there, waiting?

The police aren't looking for you anymore.

I'm not sure if they ever were looking for you, not really.

The detective only comes back because of the weans. It's a courtesy, but he brings them lollipops. He asks them about school.

He looks at them like they're orphans. As if they don't have me either.

His eyes seem to say, "what's the point of looking for a missing person who doesn't want to be found?"

You're not missing.

You're hidden.

You made sure of that.

I wish I had thought of it first.

He tilted his head back and breathed in the London
sky, raindrops pelting his closed eyelids like
midges.
He thought of home.

WILFRED

WILFRED

Two Weetabix. Skimmed milk. A Granny Smith. Builder's tea.

Wilfred's day had started this way for the past seventy years. There used to be two bowls on this table. Not anymore.

10am. Time to wash up the previous night's dishes. Original Fairy Liquid. The same sponge for the past two years. Threadbare tea towels that had survived three house moves, two children and one counter-wandering cat.

10.15am. The daily bowel movement. Andrex. Imperial Leather soap. Cold water.

Downstairs to settle into the waiting indent in the sofa cushion for the day. Opposite the accusatory presence of the telephone.

The telephone that rang every day at 10.30am.

10.30am. Six rings. A blink syncopated with each ring. Silence again.

Wilfred sighed and picked up his book in progress. Today, Churchill's *A History of the English-Speaking Peoples*. The fourth time he had read it in his lifetime.

One hour of reading. Two hours of television.

1.30pm. The post arrives. The electric bill. Advertising flyers for the local Chinese and a window cleaner.

2pm. Two slices of wholemeal bread, half a tin of baked beans. A tin of sardines. A pear.

One hour of gardening. Light spots of rain on his bare neck. Grumble "bloody weather". Back inside.

A walk to the corner shop. Two pints of milk. A loaf of bread. A scratch card, beaten with a copper and angrily tossed into the bin outside the shop.

A short conversation with Joanne. Thirty-five. Next door neighbour but one. Brown hair. Eyes that shine with a hope not yet lost. Jokes about roadworks. Affectionate smiles.

3.45pm. One crumpet. Jam.

4.12pm. Memories like a flood. The words echo, *I don't need your help*.

Alice's face, crushed by his words.

4.15pm. Back to reality. No use dwelling on the past. Milky tea and two sugars. The newspaper's crossword puzzle. Fall asleep midway.

6.42pm. Awake with a snort. Dinner. Two frozen cod pieces. Tinned marrowfat peas. A slice of bread and butter.

One hour of television. A documentary about the River Tay. Three custard creams and a final cup of tea.

8pm. The phone rings.

The phone never rings at 8pm.

Standing up to answer it is breathless work. Answered within eight rings.

"Hello?"

"Hello, Dad."

Samuel's voice.

A silence far too long.

"Hello?"

"What's wrong?"

"Everything's fine," Samuel says.

"Good."

Another silence.

"Are you okay?"

Worry in Samuel's voice. The same worry with which Alice had offered to help him out of his chair.

Take my hand, Dad.

I don't need your help.

The face she had made. Exasperation and sympathy. Pity that had made him angry.

"Are you still there?"

"Yes. I'm fine." Wilfred barked. The same anger.

"I want to visit."

"No, the drive is too far. The motorways are dangerous."

"Dad-"

"No, Samuel."

8.08pm. The call ends. A shaking hand forcibly placing down the receiver.

8.12pm. Three minutes staring at the phone. Three minutes of pounding heartbeat in his ears.

Back to the sofa. The last 45 minutes of a soap. Bath at 9pm. Bed at 9.30pm.

7am. Pain from shoulders to lower back. Must have slept funny.

Radio in bed.

Downstairs.

Two Weetabix.

Skimmed milk.

A Granny Smith.

Builder's tea.

10.30am. Those six rings. Every weekday for six months.

A breath after the sixth.

But it continues.

Seven rings.

Eight rings.

Wilfred's up before the ninth. Answered by the tenth.

"Hello?"

"You actually answered."

"Mm."

"I'm sorry for yesterday."

"Mm."

"I won't drive down if you don't want me to."

Silence.

"Look, I-"

The words are loaded with apprehension. News. Something bad has happened.

"Charlotte is pregnant."

A grandchild.

Wilfred wished Edith had been here for this news. Maybe then she could have answered the damn phone.

"Are you there?"

"A baby?"

It's a redundant phrase. But *congratulations* is too hard to say.

"Yes, a baby."

"Oh."

"Maybe we could come down on the train. After the baby is born. She's due next month."

A baby.

Alice in her cot. So small and pink. Edith, exhausted but beautiful as always. This is how he remembered them. Young. Safe.

"Charlotte had her scan. It's a girl."

"Oh."

Wilfred wanted to shout for joy. Do a little dance. Put on Buddy Holly. But he couldn't.

"I have to go now."

"Ta-ra."

2pm. A cheese sandwich.

Corner shop. Runner beans. Butter.

Joanne.

"I'm going to be a grandfather."

Congratulatory hugs. The joy of a friend's touch.

But Joanne is not Alice.

3.45pm. One crumpet. Marmite.

4.12pm. The memories come again. Samuel ringing to tell him Alice had died in a car crash. Two tears. Pain in his chest.

4.15pm. Tea. Crossword.

6.54pm. Pulled awake from the nap by hunger. Dinner. Edith's shepherd's pie. Now only four left in the freezer. Runner beans. A slice of bread and butter.

Documentary. Custard creams.

Bath. Bed.

Weetabix.

Churchill.

The phone.

Two rings.

"Hello?"

"Dad."

"Samuel."

JESS

JESS

"I just can't believe she's really gone," Martha cries against my shoulder.

"I know," I say, rubbing Martha's back, searching for the right observation to add as I listen to Martha's deep sobbing, finally landing on, "She was so young."

There's a fire dancing in front of us, tongues waving and falling as if to the rhythm of our conversation.

The heat stifles me, encasing my skin, but I can't move from this spot as Martha continues, "How could someone *do* that to her?"

I notice some of the other funeral goers, most of whom are demolishing the buffet to our right, are staring, as if Martha's grief is inappropriate. Emotion makes the English squirm, even at a funeral, the most socially acceptable place to allow such an outpouring. But they think Martha has gone too far; tears are for in private, funerals are for perfunctory gestures and giving a few coppers to the church collection plate.

I side-eye one of the older women, mindlessly putting a

samosa into her mouth whilst watching us. She averts her gaze as I meet her eyes and I shake my head slightly.

I don't mind Martha's grief. It feels nice that someone is mourning Jess.

"Can I get you a glass of water?" Dawn, Jess' mother, says quietly, coming to crouch by Martha's side, "Or a cup of tea?"

Martha is too busy wailing, but I nod to Dawn and mouth a thank you. Martha doesn't seem to notice the absurdity of the deceased's mother bringing *her* a glass of water. After all, she only knew Jess in passing. They were in the same department at work but they were hardly friends.

"Thea," my name is said by way of greeting, in a way that makes me want to screw up my mouth, and Jack Piper claps a hand against my back, "I haven't seen you in ages. At least a couple of decades, I think."

He comes round in front of the fire, towering over Martha and I on the settee. He must be eighty-five now, but he doesn't look much different to how I remember him.

We were in a play together once – I, then thirty-something, was the Desdemona to his Othello. Jess had played Emilia in the same production and though she was my age, thirty years his junior, he had repeatedly made advances towards her, leading to her eventually leaving the theatre company to avoid him. He's barely an acquaintance; he shouldn't be here, but I'm not surprised that he is. He never had much self-awareness.

"Jack," I reply quietly, mimicking his greeting, straining to make eye contact and keep my arms around Martha.

"How are you?" he asks, a playful smirk on his lips as his eyes flit from my face to my chest and back up again.

"I'm well, apart from the obvious," I say, gesturing to the setting. I release my hold on Martha as I see Jack isn't intending to leave us alone anytime soon and turn to face him a little more. I hope he can see the disdain in my eyes.

"Oh yes, terrible news, terrible news," Jack says dismissively, slurping his whiskey, scrambling for a platitude and adding: "She was the life and soul of the party!"

I 'mm' in response, hoping he will leave us alone, but he doesn't, "Have they found out who did it yet?"

I looked around to try to indicate he should keep his voice down but he's oblivious.

"Jesus Christ. No," I hiss.

"What a tragedy," Jack muses, this entire event a play to which he is merely the audience, "Aren't you going to ask how I am, Thea?"

"How are you, Jack?" I spit out reluctantly.

"I'm doing fantastically. Did you hear I'm playing the ghost in *Hamlet* this season?" My mouth opens and closes incredulously, but he isn't finished, "Robert's playing my son."

I have to restrain a snort, firstly at the titular role of *Hamlet* being described as "my son", as if the play was actually about the ghost of Old Hamlet, barely popping into the plot, and secondly, at imagining Robert, only three years younger than Jack, playing a thirty-year old.

"Oh," I reply, Dawn returning with Martha's water. She shoots Jack a look which he either ignores or is too self-absorbed to notice. Martha feverishly gulps the water through shoulder-shaking sniffles.

"Jess loved Shakespeare," Martha says into her empty cup.

"Yes, she did," Jack agrees jovially, "Did you know we played lovers on the stage?"

Seeing Martha's face light up at the opportunity to talk more about Jess (being unaware of who Jack is), I take the chance to leave, slinking over to the buffet.

"I'll be right back," I say to Martha, but she's not listening. Her eyes are fixed on Jack as he puffs out his chest and commences the story.

"Thea," Akash nods a forced greeting as I grab a paper plate.

"Nice to see you, Akash. I'm sorry for your loss," I say politely. He has always hated me. Perhaps because mine and Jess' friendship was always so close. I knew her first.

He wrinkles his nose at my obvious insincerity before snapping, "Just leave me alone, yeah?"

He grabs his plate, having to scoop up the edge with his palm as the pile he's mindlessly spooned on flops to the side, and walks away. I doubt he'll take a single bite.

As he passes her, the older woman who was staring at Martha earlier raises her eyebrow at me, but I avert my eyes, placing salad onto my paper plate.

"Jess was so lucky to have you," Dawn says, coming over to top up one of the crisp bowls. She hasn't stopped all day.

"That's sweet," I gently smile, conscious of my tone after my run-ins with Akash and Jack. I reach for a piece of bread and add it awkwardly onto my mound of salad.

"Would you mind...?" Dawn starts, thinly masked emotion in her voice, "Could you speak to my mother?"

Jess' grandmother? I try to remember if I have ever met her before. The thought of meeting more family fills me with dread. Having Martha cry on me was enough for one day.

Dawn must have seen the blank look on my face because she adds, "Jess talked about you a lot. She just wants to hear some of your stories."

"Oh," I say, lips flapping. How do you say no to someone who is grieving? Her entire face is a map of Jess' life, fallen and wrinkled with the knowledge that it was cut short. She's sentenced to this new life forever. A life without Jess.

I watch her eyes as I reluctantly nodded, the desperate joy of knowing I will fulfil her request burning a fire in them that for a brief moment burns brighter than the pain.

"This way," she says, leading me through to the kitchen

where Jess' grandmother is sat at the table speaking to another family member.

"Mother, this is Thea," Dawn says, placing a hand gently but firmly against the small of my back to encourage me into the chair opposite Jess' grandmother. "Thea, this is my mother - Rosemary."

"Beautiful service, wasn't it?" Rosemary says.

Dawn is a mirror of her mother, and for the first time I see a lot of Jess in both of their faces. I swallow tensely and try to give a small smile.

"Yes, it was," I say, wondering if it would be impolite to eat the piece of baguette on my plate, "Very moving," I add.

It's a lie.

I stood at the altar. I walked with the coffin. I sat in the pews and held people's hands.

I felt raw and alone, but I didn't feel moved.

"How did you know Jess?" Rosemary asked.

"Mother," Dawn says patiently, "This is *Thea*. Jess' friend from Nightingale."

"Oh!" Rosemary says, a look of recognition sparking in her eyes, "Nightingale – the acting school? You were with her at The Queen's Head weren't you? The night that she..."

"That's right," I say, and we both share a look that indicates neither of us want to dwell on that detail.

"She spoke about you all the time," Rosemary states, as though she's proud to have finally met me.

She's looking up at Dawn, whose face has been shrouded with pain at mention of her daughter's last day. A corkscrew of pressure builds at the back of my throat. I can't fall apart. I just have to breathe through it.

The uncomfortable pause I'm creating is beginning to stretch across the room between the four of us. I blink away the stinging feeling in my eyelids as I search for words less provoking than the first ones that spring to mind.

Rosemary looked at her hands. I wonder if she knew why Jess was at The Queen's Head that night. Or if the police know what she did when she left.

That thought eases the twisting feeling in my oesophagus.

"You knew each other a long time," Rosemary says, desperate to prompt me into speaking, "You must have some amazing stories."

"Uh, yes..." I say, picking at a piece of lettuce tentatively. It's hard to look her in the eye. There was so much of Jess in the way she focussed on my face, an attentiveness that she has.

Had.

"Although no drunken misadventures," Rosemary chides, "I hear there were many, but I'd rather not know."

I purse my lips slightly at the perceived dig at me. How much does she really know about that night?

"I have other stories," I say stonily, "It wasn't *all* drunken nights–"

I'm cut off as Mike appears in the doorway between the kitchen and the entrance hall. He gestures to follow him. His eyes say it's not a request.

Dawn notices his flailing waves, "A friend of yours?" she asks me. She's naïve that presence could be anything threatening; Jess was well-loved and so the funeral was an open house.

"My brother – he was in the year above at Nightingale actually," I say, Dawn and Rosemary nodding as if they remember him. I add, "Please excuse me."

I try to breath deeply to avoid looking too stiff as I walk out of the room, but my lungs aren't inflating evenly, and I know I must look juddery. Hopefully they will pass that off as grief.

It wasn't the anger on his face that bothered me. Mike's like me – rage first, ask questions later.

But the fear in his eyes has me panicked.

I hurry out of the room, to find him waiting for me in the front garden. He's leaning against the wall of the house, head rhythmically knocking against it.

There are cars circling out of the huge driveway, the noise of their tyres against the puddle-filled gravel roaring louder than it should in my ears. Mourners who feel they have done their share. They've earned some time at home, away from the anguish of Jess' loved ones.

I envy their freedom.

I approach Mike, hoping he'll stop tilting his head up and look at me. Anxiety radiates from him.

Although it's not raining anymore, the leaves above us have been saturated. They can't take anymore and ooze their burdens down onto us.

"Mike?" I say, my voice not my own. It rasps in shame.

I wait for him to speak, heart fluttering up and down my left side.

"Is it true?" he says.

My body crumples against my will and I have to place my palm against the bricks.

He knows.

I killed Jess.

UNDEVELOPED HISTORY

UNDEVELOPED HISTORY

I wonder for a moment if I'm going to collapse right here on the pavement. My heartbeat fills my ears, and my clenched jaw brings a sharp pain to my temples.

I roll up my sleeves.

A raindrop sliding down my now naked right forearm distracts me. I watch it as it slaloms between my arms hairs. They're stood on end.

I smooth them down and under my breath I practice what I'm going to say, as if perfecting my rehearsed words would lend my physical body some support.

I hadn't truly imagined myself here, taking in the brick walls, the sunflowers that always drooped to the left of the kitchen window, the broken bench that Dad had never gotten around to fixing. It was all still here along with my memory of it, barely changed by the new owner.

How tranquil it is now, and how stained it is in my memory. I see it all with the haze of my childhood's eyes. The terror of it sends a chill through me.

Before I lose my nerve, I stride to the front door and use the knocker.

The door starts to open and an elderly woman shuffles into view.

"Hello?"

"Good afternoon, Mrs. Horton," I say, rattling through the words I scripted for myself cheerily. I can see she's immediately put at ease by my tone as I continue, "I'm from AgeAid. My boss, Angela, called you on Monday to say I'd be coming?"

"Oh, Angela, yes," she says, "She said she was coming on Saturday?"

"It is Saturday today," I say, a gentle chuckle hiding any guilt I feel about lying to her. I know from reading her son's emails that Angela will be in for a shift tomorrow. I also know that Mrs. Horton doesn't know what day it is. I read weeks of email chains and they all concurred that on weekdays, AgeAid rarely sends someone to help her. That's something that upsets Simon, her son. Not that he offers to help her out himself. I add with a breezy air, "The weekends come around so quickly don't they?"

"Yes," Mrs. Horton says, eyebrows raised, but not seeming to doubt me. I'm ashamed as I realise that it's herself that she's doubting, "The days blur into one," she adds, sadness and confusion clouding her words, "Is Angela ill?"

"No, but I'm new so... I'm Lucy," I reply, thinking on my feet. I'm certain she doesn't know who I am, but I still need to be careful, so I don't give her my real name.

"Oh," she says, nodding slowly. She doesn't ask for ID, she simply says, "Do come in," she adds.

"Have you had any visitors today?" I ask, wanting to be sure we're alone.

"Well, my son used to come around a lot," she says, and I follow her into the hallway, wiping my shoes on the mat but leaving them on, "But he's so busy with work and the kids now. He comes by on my birthday and Mother's Day though, every year!"

I bite my lip. Hold your nerve, I remind myself.

"Oh, that's good," I say casually, looking around. The hallway is different – it's been fitted with a handle for Mrs. Horton, I presume because she is unsteady on her feet. The iron grey and navy-blue floral wallpaper is mostly covered by photo collages of her family. I recognise her son from his email account's photo. He looks just like her.

The adult me is glad that she has fittings to help her live more comfortably, but the child in me hates the changes. I notice the subtlest differences, things I hadn't thought about since I was ten, but now remember so vividly.

As she leads me into the living room my hand sweeps the doorframe. The pencil marks Mum had drawn to measure my height are gone, painted over in a bright white, a blank page for someone else's kids.

The changes in the living room hit me hard. The carpet is the same although darker with age, but the room somehow looks smaller. Our sofas are gone, Dad's armchair, my bean bag. I don't know why that surprises me, but I can feel their absence in the room. Instead is a hospital-style bed, bright white sheets and handsets with large buttons.

"I had to move down here last year after I broke my hip," Mrs. Horton explains, "I can't use the stairs anymore."

"You couldn't get a stairlift?" I ask quietly.

She smiles gently and says, "AgeAid pushed to get me on the waiting list, but they said not to get my hopes up. There are so many people on the list."

"I'm sorry about that," I say.

"Did you not bring any shopping?" She says, gesturing to my empty hands.

"Shopping?" I ask. The email had said Angela would leave enough food for the entire week. I have to make conscious effort to control my facial expressions, so she doesn't notice that I'm panicking.

I could have just explained it all to her, asked her if I could come in. But then I would have had to tell her who I am. Who my dad is.

"Angela usually brings shopping, for the dinner?" she says, frustration moving across the lines of her lips.

"Angela said the ingredients would be waiting for me."

"She never brings me what I want," Mrs. Horton replies and I'm ashamed of myself for not thinking to bring her something, even if that isn't the reason I'm here. "I don't have much in," she says, hobbling towards the kitchen, using the walls to keep her balance.

I have no qualms about cooking for her, but I can't think how I'm going to get upstairs. When I read the email to Simon from Angela about 'house services' I presumed it had meant cleaning the house, not cooking.

Mrs. Horton goes through the fridge, taking out some packaged bacon, half-used cream, some vegetables and eggs.

I join her in rummaging through her cupboards and freezer, not finding much besides ready meals, tea bags and bourbon biscuits. It's not just the kitchen of someone who can't cook for themselves, but also of someone who always eats alone. Individual portions of frozen shepherd's pie stare up at me from the freezer drawer and I close my eyes for a moment.

I thought I could just pop in and out of her life, not think about who she is actually is. But I can't help wanting to help her.

I close the freezer and comb through the drawers. A packet of spaghetti is buried at the back of one of them, a few months out of date.

"Carbonara?" I suggest.

"Do you know how to make that?" She says, surprised and impressed in equal measure.

I imagine her, alone with a ready meal and a cup of tea. I croak out, "Yes, I do."

I still don't know how I'll get upstairs as planned. I presumed I'd be dusting or scrubbing the bath by now, the perfect cover to move around the house as needed. Maybe I can find an excuse to use the upstairs bathroom.

I boil water. Create the sauce. Dig through the cupboards for herbs. I was just a kid when I lived here, so I'd never cooked at this stove, but even so, standing in front of it I feel my mum, her ghost cooking along with me.

Mrs. Horton lays the kitchen table with cutlery, two plates and coasters. She may not have many guests, but she takes care over every part of the table.

"We need napkins," she says quietly, leaning her weight against the table and frowning.

"Kitchen paper?" I say, brandishing the roll.

"No, no, cloth ones," she says as I drain the pasta and combine it with the sauce, "But they're in the airing cupboard."

My ears prick. I know where the airing cupboard is.

Upstairs.

"I'll go and grab them," I say, slightly too eagerly. Mrs. Horton doesn't notice.

"If that would be okay, dear," she says, sitting at one side of the table.

I turn off the burner.

"I won't be a second," I say with a smile, turning towards the hallway.

"It's at the top of the stairs, the cupboard to your left," she calls to me as I approach the bottom of the stairs and I chide myself for not thinking to ask. She doesn't seem suspicious of me, but I want to make this as smooth as possible.

"Thank you!" I reply.

I place a hand on the banister and the muscle memory comes back to me. How each foot takes my weight, the distance between each step, the grip of the varnished wood under my fingertips. How many times did I climb these stairs? Grounded for making a mess, going to bed early with toothache, taking them two at a time to outrun my dad.

I swallow a hard ball of emotion and continue. Concentrate, I urge myself.

There's the airing cupboard, and I go to it first as I'm worried that I'll forget otherwise. The smell is different as I pull open the doors. I hope for the waft of clean towels, my mum's perfume seeming to perforate every item of clothing and bedsheet. But all that hits me is stale air and the over-powering scent of rose fabric softener.

I grab the cloth napkins and close the airing cupboard quietly.

I know my parents' old room is right behind me, but I can't look, skirting past the bathroom door to my old room first.

To call it a junk room would be compassionate – it is a rubbish mound. I can barely make out my yellow walls for the piles of magazines, bulk toilet paper, bin bags full of clothes and dusty pieces of living room furniture stacked precariously on top of each other. It surprises me that the rest of the house doesn't look like this, but I expect this was where Mrs. Horton's son shoved everything when they moved the hospital bed into the front room. It's a sad capsule of her life, unloved objects and forgotten collections jumbled into a cramped space.

I was hoping to feel something looking at this room, but I don't. I'm struggling to remember what it looked like when I lived here. My bed was against the far wall, I remember that much, but where was my toybox? Bright green with paint handprints on it. I think my dad made it for me.

"Have you got them?" Mrs. Horton says.

"Still looking," I lie, leaning against the doorway of my old room.

I breathe deeply and turn towards my parents' room. I have a far more complete version of this room held in my head, possibly because of the amount of time I spent in here with mum, painting or drawing. Their bed used to be in the centre of the room, headboard against the window so that the sun peaking under the curtain would wake them.

My mum's desk had been against the left-hand wall, always cluttered with paper, paints and pencils, scattered and disordered, at least to an outsider. She always knew where everything was.

The room is pretty empty now, I guess because Mrs. Horton was using it as her main bedroom before she moved downstairs, and all that's left is a frayed armchair where my parents' bed used to be and a few boxes of books and video tapes.

I walk further into the room and face the right-hand wall. The chip in the paint is still there from my dad's ring, where it had ricocheted and slammed into the plasterboard. I trace my eyes down from that mark, memories welling in my eyes.

The stain's not there anymore. Perhaps Mrs. Horton changed the carpet when she moved in, or maybe the police sorted it when they found my mum's body. A professional cleaning. One of those big machines. I can't be sure, because the carpet is the same light beige that it was years ago.

I walk over to the spot and kneel down, running my fingers through the fibres. If it is the same carpet, I can't find any trace of her left. It's immaculate, like new.

I stifle my sobs as I lean my back against the wall, gripping the napkins hard to stop myself crying out. I inhale through the shakes and focus. I switch back to my knees and lift up the corner of the carpet where it comes away from the skirting board.

The wooden floor beneath is the same, and I run my fingers along the joins until I find the correct floorboard, prising it up with my fingertips.

I start sobbing anew. They're all still here.

I take them out and shove them into my bra, the only place I can think to hide them.

"Mrs. Horton?" I hear a woman's voice from downstairs and my heart stops.

"Angela?" Mrs. Horton replies.

She's slowly shuffling into the living room, the soft drag of her slippers filling the silence as I wait to hear Angela speak again.

"Hello, Mrs. Horton, I used my key, I hope that's okay?"

"Of course, dear," Mrs. Horton replies, "But I thought you sent someone else today – she's made me dinner."

Oh god.

I get up, walking as quietly as I can back down the stairs, cloth napkins still in hand. The front door isn't an option, but I know that the utility room behind the stairs has a door that goes into the back garden.

"No – me again!" Angela says, apparently not taking note of what Mrs. Horton has said about the dinner.

I tiptoe out of the hallway, leaving the napkins on the stairs and trying to edge through the dining room to the utility room.

They've both become quiet, but I can hear Angela clattering in the kitchen. She must be looking over the meal I made and trying to put the pieces together.

"Did you make this?" she asks, clearly confused.

"No, your girl did," Mrs. Horton says, frustration ebbing through.

"My girl..."

"The one from AgeAid, she said you sent her. She went upstairs to get some napkins."

"Right," Angela says, "I better go and talk to her because I didn't send anyone."

This is my only chance to get out. I gently push open the utility room door. I stop – it's a mess, stuff piled up to the backdoor. I start to step over the bin bags, boxes and clothes.

"Hello?"

I hear Angela start to walk up the stairs and I freeze, worried she's heard me moving around, but her footsteps disappear over my head, walking around the upstairs rooms. I have minutes at most before she heads back down.

I move faster, tripping over a box of dishware and nearly falling, grabbing one of the counters. I stop, worried I've made a noise, but neither Angela nor Mrs. Horton indicate that they've heard me.

I make it to the door and I can hear Angela walking into the bathroom directly above me. I gently lower the handle - the door is locked.

God, oh god. I can barely think. Maybe I could explain my reasons for being here, but the lie is too deep, they would definitely call the police.

Footsteps above me.

Think.

We used to keep the key in the drawer above the washing machine. I jump back over the piles, not thinking about the noise anymore.

Angela is descending the stairs now, going back to the Mrs. Horton.

"There's no one up there," she says gently, in the sort of patronising tone that people use with older women, as if she's a child, "What did she say her name was?"

"I can't remember," Mrs. Horton says. I can hear the fear

in her voice as her own mind betrays her. I feel awful thinking that Angela and others won't believe her when she tells this story, that she'll be doubted, made to feel senile.

I open the drawer and rifle through screwdrivers, old batteries and appliance manuals.

There's a mint tin at the back that rattles as I pick it up and I open it. There's the key.

"There's really nobody else here, Mrs. Horton – are you sure you saw someone?" Angela says again and I want to run back in there and slap her for her condescension.

"She made me *dinner*," Mrs. Horton says indignantly, "She went upstairs to get napkins."

I'm back over the piles of junk, key in hand.

"Well, I'll go and get some napkins and we can enjoy the food, shall we?" Angela says. Mrs. Horton replies with an exasperated sigh.

I'm fiddling with the key in the lock, trying to swallow my fear and guilt.

I hear Angela walk into the hallway, "Hang on," she says, "Isn't this door usually shut?"

I hear her walk into the utility room just as I start to scale the garden fence, gripping the trellis to haul myself over the other side. The neighbour's garden is big and there's no one here to see me, so I crouch down behind the fence.

Angela opens the back door and looks out into the garden. Not seeing anything, she heads back inside, and I run, climbing the next few fences until I reach the road and sprint back to where I left my car.

Dad hated photos. Not just of him, of any of us. The only photo I have of the three of us is from my fifth birthday party, one that gran took covertly and developed for me. I wonder if she knew that day, when she got us to stand together, what her son was doing behind closed doors.

When gran passed away, she left me her camera, an old SLR, before the days of digital, but perfectly good. It had three rolls of film left in the case and I used them sparingly, knowing even if I saved every penny of my pocket money, I wouldn't be able to afford any more. I would sneak photos, especially of mum, but I couldn't afford to get them developed so I would put them under the floorboard when dad was at work.

I don't know if mum knew that I hid them in there, but she hid the camera for me in one of her shoeboxes in the back of her wardrobe. As far as I know, dad never knew it was there.

When the police came, called by the neighbours I presume, social services grabbed a few teddies, some clothes, my trainers, the basics. I was told years later that I didn't speak for a week after it happened, and no doubt I didn't tell the social worker about these rolls of film. My parents' room was a crime scene, cordoned off as I was hurried out of the house catching a glimpse of the red permeating into the carpet under my mum's head.

But all three rolls were still there. There's no way Mrs. Horton would have known they were there when she bought the house.

I take out one of the rolls and gently pull the tab to unfurl it, looking through the negatives. They're small and dark but there she is. A face I haven't seen in seventeen years, smiling up at me from her art desk as she sweeps paint across a piece of paper.

My mum.

She's with me now as I walk home, shielding the
  photographs from the rain in the folds of my
  jacket.
Her smile is on my face.

THE WEIGHT OF RAIN

THE WEIGHT OF RAIN

I have never noticed how trees weep when it rains before. But that day every tree in the cemetery shed tears of opalescent misery. Each bead felt like extra weight as they ran from the branches above and onto my head.

The rain was temporary, the misery was not. By the time the coffin was being lowered into the ground, the sun was mocking me with its optimism.

Cora was my mentor. I say that without any bitterness for the clichés that surround that term. The word is fitting for her, her experience, her effortlessly wise advice and her wit in the face of harsh reality.

The day I met Cora was punishing. After six hours at the office I waited forty-seven minutes in the most dismal and stinging rain for a train to arrive. The droplets were so cold that they hit my face like needles. The train finally arrived, and I was given brief respite from the cold as it whisked me to my destination – London.

London was and is my least favourite place to be, but I spent many days there with Cora seeing the beauty of a metropolitan world through her eyes.

I was late for the rock concert by the time my train pulled in and so I ran the entire way from Waterloo station to the tiny theatre in Soho, rummaging my bag for my presumably lost ticket as I crossed the bridge.

I knew my boss would be furious if I missed this and I was fully prepared to write anything in my review, even if fictitious, to avoid her ever finding out.

I slipped in, brandishing my press ticket to eye-rolling attendants as I found a seat right at the back, not wanting to draw the attention of the band by attempting to search for D14, an allusive number, no doubt positioned preposterously close to the potentially peeved musicians.

My buttocks had barely been acquainted with the seat when a confident voice whispered to me, "No one is ever late to a performance darling, not even the band, who got here only moments before you."

I turned and met the eyes of my comforter, bewildered and grateful in equal measure. I clocked my rumpled dress, sweaty armpits and no doubt unruly hair and began to dread making a friend on such an abysmal day. She, however – Cora, as I'm sure you guessed – was flawless. Audacious. Bonkers. Her eyes were lit with an unextinguishable fire for life and in that moment that was my drug. It was exactly what I needed.

"They're drunk out of their minds - look!"

She chortled, gesturing to the lead guitarist who was struggling with his own guitar neck like a child learning to hold a pen for the first time. I quickly took out my notebook and scribbled down something amusing about drunken men and large members which produced a genuine snort from Cora.

"A reporter?" she asked, noting my press ticket as she nursed a pint of beer.

"Not a very good one." I whispered back, realising that whilst the band may have been oblivious to our conversation, some of the people seated in front of us were starting to turn their heads.

"As if a writer is able to judge their own merit." Cora said assertively.

"What does that mean?" I hissed back, confusion and the frustration of the day combining to make more heat in my tone than I intended.

"Every writer thinks they are appalling, even if they say otherwise."

She said this with a wry smile as if she knew more than she was saying (which, I later learned, she did. She knew all there was to know).

We talked for hours, barely aware of the droning presence of the concert. She was instantly my best friend, but I ultimately knew that she was like this with everyone; she was the type of person to charm the devil: a natural smooth talker.

Stood underneath the rain-weighted trees at her funeral years later, I felt her absence like a shackle around my ankle. I hadn't realised that the shackle was of my own making and had existed for my entire life until I met her. It wasn't the droplets of rain that weighed me down, nor the slowly descending coffin, but my own triviality in a world where someone like Cora could, and had, existed. She said awful things to me, as any friend should be able to. She tore me down when I was arrogant, and she built me up when I was unsure.

She didn't live to see me write my first novel, but the day I met her I graduated from music critic to novelist, at least in my own mind. That's the power that worshipping someone grants, and now I must live with my grief and my own inadequacy.

HENNA

HENNA

WatWace were a terrible rock band, a jumbled line up of has-beens, used-to-be-famouses and over-inflated egos. A friend of mine, Roo, was a cult fan of WatWace, finding the seriousness with which they regarded their truly awful music to be an endless supply of entertainment. Said friend was travelling in Italy during WatWace's London tour, but I decided to book myself onto every single show of theirs in a strange act of masochism, praying that the so-bad-its-good factor was as potent as promised.

On the day I met Henna, the band were booked to play a small London theatre, a dingy little place built in an old library, with two hundred or so seats crammed in next to each other. I noticed Henna before she'd even sat down, slipping in through a side door after the band had already come out onto the stage, waving her ticket in a flapping and frantic motion.

I smiled to myself as I noted her snaking through the sea of knees towards the empty seat next to me. She was my sort of person. In that series of panicked microgestures I could see her genuineness oozing out of every pore like sunbeams.

We were destined to be friends, all I had to do was speak.

"No one is ever really late to a performance, darling, not even the band, who got here only moments before you," I whispered, hoping humour was the right tone to wash away the mortified pink that was crowding her cheeks.

She was immaculately dressed, smoothing down the edges of her floral dress almost unconsciously, retroactively ironing out her embarrassment. She was insecure, I could see that in the way she wouldn't leave her hair alone – delicate and shiny but frazzled from her rush to get in.

"They're drunk out of their minds, look!" I said, keeping my tone light as I gestured to the lead guitarist, burping down his beer and fumbling to find the chords.

That was enough to cool her off – I could see the cogs whirring behind her eyes as she took out a well-worn notebook and wrote:

As the much-mocked WatWace take to the stage, two-time GRAMMY winner Lawrence Rolebourne drunkenly wrestles with his guitar neck like an elephant using its trunk for the first time. If the rumours of his well-endowed member are to be taken literally, I would hate to see the state of the urinal floor in the backstage area after the show.

It was a corny line, but I could see how pleased she was with it and so I forced a tuft of air through my nose in encouragement as I read it over her shoulder. Her face lit up a little. I could see this was her passion.

My favourite thing is finding someone who has a passion – a real one, not these wankers who go on about their "passion for working in high-paced work environments" on LinkedIn – and asking them about it.

Their mouths flicker neon bright as they implore you to love it as much as they do. Of course, I never quite share their enthusiasm, but the buzz of lighting that match and watching the flash travel through their entire being is a high of its own.

"A reporter?" I asked, grabbing my beer and taking a rather foamy sip.

"Not a very good one," she whispered back. I hear a woman behind us tut; our conversation is rudely interrupting the band screaming out "Plump Woman". Roo was right about their so-bad-it's-good-ness.

I paused for a moment. The way she replied makes me think this is what she says every time she's asked about her job. It's automatic. Hard-wired self-flagellation.

"As if a writer is able to judge their own merit," I replied.

I was her once. Perhaps not quite as dejected – my arrogance carried me through – but it was a mask that I wore to hide my inadequacy. Or so I thought.

"What does that mean?" she said. There was fear behind her eyes that made her look angry. She quickly looked away; she couldn't hold eye contact with me. She was afraid I'd see into her.

I leant back and sighed.

"Every writer thinks they are appalling," I started.

"But I actually am," Henna said, blinking at the page in front of her.

"No, you just think you are," I mused, "It's a terrible paradox. We see other people, the people we admire, doing something we think is so far away from what we could never achieve it, that we stop trying. The truth is, they all think they're shit too."

"No, no, I know what you mean – imposter syndrome," Henna said.

"I've not heard of that," I laughed, eliciting another tut from the woman behind us, "But that sounds like it."

"But that's not me, I actually am a sham. I didn't get the job on merit."

"Well, I don't know about that - I wasn't there - but does it matter how you got the job? You're doing it."

"I'm not successful. I'm just writing for a shitty magazine," she said. I was surprised at her insistence. This was more than ingrained self-loathing, this was practised. She had honed it for conversations such as this; none of it was conscious.

"And since when does success equal skill?" I said.

"Well, of course it does! What's the point of skill if no one else recognises it?"

"Look at these idiots," I chuckled, both hands gesturing at the stage, "They're famous, they're successful. They've got merchandise lining the entrance halls. Those t-shirts are going for twenty quid. All of that, and yet they are truly atrocious."

The woman behind me gave a final, over-exaggerated tut and stood up from her seat. I was vaguely aware of her and her companion shuffling past the other fans to find somewhere else to sit as I continued, "Does other people's view of your success control how you think about yourself?"

She didn't know how to reply to that. I don't know if she had ever truly considered that she was living to other people's standards.

She pursed her lips, moving her pen across the bottom corner of the page as if testing it for ink. I would later find this to be a nervous tick of hers.

"I'm Cora," I said quietly, trying to bring her back to the conversation.

"Henna," she answered, with a flash of a smile at the corner of her mouth. I started to think I pushed it too far – she wasn't ready for me to bring her world view into question, we had only just met.

But then, she surprised me. She showed me a hint of the true Henna, buried under layers of taught suppression.

"I don't want to live for other people," she murmured, still unable to look me in the eye. She cleared her throat and then somewhat more confidently said, "I'm afraid, but I can't stop writing."

The conversation flowed easily after that point.

She told me about her childhood, born to a Bangladeshi mother and a French father in East London. She had a huge family spread across two continents. Four sisters, all of whom had gotten married in their twenties and had children shortly after. She spoke of their different world views, their squabbles, their love for one another.

She felt like the family disappointment, rejecting ideas of settling down into married life in order to pursue a career.

I empathised.

There's scorn for childless women.

In my twenties, I was told I would change my mind. In my thirties, I was pitied and told it was "not too late". By the time I hit forty-five, there was nothing left but hatred, whether out of jealousy or misunderstanding, I'm not sure.

"My sisters think I don't understand the world because I haven't had children," Henna said a few hours into our conversation. The band were still droning on, and she had been alternating between our chat and scrawling down savagely hilarious reviews of the songs.

"Why do you think they view you that way?" I asked, trying to spur her on a little. The more we talked, the more I found she had the tools to push past her lack of self-esteem. There was a lot more to her than that.

"I think I scare them," she replied, "I have autonomy."

Those words have stuck with me to this day.

"Do you think they don't have autonomy?" I replied, trying to keep my tone impartial.

"To some extent," she said, tucking one leg under her and shifting her weigh onto the arm rest nearest to me, still doodling her pen against the bottom right corner of the note-book. It was scratched with endless overlapping black lines, her fingertips sticky with residue. "They joke that they envy me," she continued, "But it's like a secret club. They want me to be part of it, or they want me to be excluded from it. They don't know how to reconcile me being part of the family without sharing that part of it – the having children part."

"Being a sister and an aunt doesn't get you in – you have to be a mother too," I elucidate from my own experience of it.

"Exactly. It's an arcane understanding. The wisdom of motherhood. I know why they think that – I see what they go through. The pain and the joy. But I wish they would respect my decision, as I've respected theirs."

We went on to talk about loss.

An aunt lost in childbirth. Her grandmother lost to cancer. And finally, her friend lost to suicide.

I felt guilty then for creating a friendship with her, knowing she would lose me too.

"I didn't mourn any of them," Henna said. By this point, we had left the theatre and were walking through a Hyde Park, the evening light fading through the tall buildings around us. Despite the sun, a few spots of rain hit our fore-arms as our elbows brushed against each other.

"Why not?" I asked.

"I couldn't," she replied, "It was too hard. I felt guilty for grieving – as if that solidified their deaths. I thought grief would be automatic. But it wasn't. I had pushed it all down too much. When I found Anita, after she had taken the pills, I just felt empty. And not feeling anything – that made me feel even more guilty."

"You really give yourself a hard time," I said.

"No, I..." she started, but she stopped herself. She knew I was right.

We continued on and found a bar.

It was dingy and smelt of bleach, a faux lemon aura of cheap booze and must.

The bartender brought us a cocktail menu and we worked our way through it along with some olives and a bread board, obnoxiously served on a wooden plank.

"Are you happy writing for the magazine?" I asked, a few cocktails in and inhibitions very much lowered.

"Yes," Henna replied, her confidence similarly bolstered by the alcohol, "Well... it's just a job, but I don't hate it."

"Is 'not hating it' the only qualifier for a job?"

"I don't want my job to define me."

"Then don't let it. But that doesn't mean you can't find something you'd rather be doing. What made you want to write for a magazine?"

"I knew the previous editor at university. He gave me some freelance articles, and before I knew it, I was full time."

"But what did you want to do before that?"

"Write novels," she said, bolting down another drink.

"Then why not do that instead?"

"Because that's just a dream," she replied with a laugh.

"And? Anything is a dream until we make it happen."

"Oh, come on," Henna laughed, "That's cheesy."

"Really cheesy," I laughed, "But true."

"I can't just quit my job and write a book," Henna said.

"Well, how about not quitting your job and writing a book?" I countered, playfully throwing a crumb at her.

She scrunched up her nose and fumbled her bottom lip against her teeth thoughtfully.

"Nah," she said, "You're funny."

We fell into vodka-soaked laughter, soon forgetting the serious topics we had blasted through.

The walls were decorated with tiles, each one clumsily painted with names. Although most of the wall behind the bar was covered with them, there were gaps, and the highest part of the wall was mostly empty. We asked the bartender, and he said visitors – usually tourists – could paint a tile and they would stick it on the wall.

A tenner later and we were smearing red paint across a tile, ineptly trying to paint each other's names, but we were laughing so raucously neither of us could keep the brushes down smoothly.

The final result was a mess, but we proudly handed it over to the bartender who gave us a disapproving look. He showed us where it would go after it had been glazed and fired – between "Emily LUVS Daniel" and the edge of the shelves that held the mixers. We quickly forgot about it, staying at the bar for a few more hours before I escorted Henna to the tube to get back home.

Four years later, there are more tiles on the wall, barely any blue squares of paint left.

"Vodka and coke, please," I say to the woman behind the bar.

I'm alone this time, phone on the damp beermat in front of me.

I choose a bar stool directly opposite the mixers. Our tile, still next to "Emily LUVS Daniel", is staring back at me.

"Here you go. £3.50," the barmaid says, handing me the vodka and coke. I pay with my phone. "Thanks," she says, leaving me to my drink. As I pull back the phone from the card machine, I notice the text.

Henna, 8.05pm
Book cover ready, what do you think? How are you?

I open the attachment. The book cover loads – a local artist had painted a minimalist version of Henna's head, side-on with her black hair spun up into an elaborate bun. I tear up as I look it over and type out:

Cora, 8.11pm
Beautiful, looks just like you.

I have a difficult phone call to make. Even more difficult given her elation about the cover.

How can I tell her I'm dying?

THE BEACH AT RINMORE POINT

THE BEACH AT RINMORE POINT

Cathryn awoke with a furious headache. She had only managed to get an hour or two of sleep for the fifth night that week.

There was no point staying in bed now – she knew she wouldn't get back to sleep.

She went to the bathroom and leaned on the edge of the sink, scrutinising herself in the mirror. Her eyes were puffy and bloodshot, and she thought how thin she looked. Once, her cheeks had been full, bouncing with laughter and love. Now she looked gaunt. This job was killing her.

After half an hour of staggering around the bedroom trying to put any type of clothing on, she rang John and told him she wouldn't be coming in.

"Oh no, is it flu?" he said, genuine concern in his voice.

"Oh, maybe, I'm sure I'll be okay in a few days," Cathryn said, making her voice sound as weak as possible, tucking her phone between her jaw and her shoulder and pouring herself a strong cup of coffee. She knew he wouldn't understand that she was "just" tired. Being burnt out was no excuse in his mind – they all were.

"Feel better soon," John said.

Cathryn's shame at having lied to him coupled with her sleep deprived state to make sure she felt truly awful about herself.

She realised as she walked around the house that Natalie hadn't woken her, as she usually did, to get the kids ready for school. The kitchen was a mess of washing up, cereal bowls and crumb-filled chopping boards.

She wondered if Natalie was angry at her for being up so late. It felt as though Natalie allowing her the lie-in was some form of judgemental punishment for Cathryn's body's dysfunction. Natalie had always been a good sleeper and she had never understood how Cathryn wouldn't feel tired until dawn most nights. It was a sore point in their marriage and always had been.

She retreated to bed with her coffee and hoped an hour or two of TV would leave her with less guilt. Or at the very least, less pain in her head.

Cathryn opened her eyes to the sound of the doorbell. She must have managed to doze off. The TV was still on, but the show had changed from a repeat of *Dr. Phil* to the RTÉ News. She groaned, and rolled out of the bed, putting her slippers on and shuffling down the stairs to answer the door.

She could see in the frosted glass that it was Mrs. Jones from next door, and she rolled her eyes before unlatching the door chain. No doubt it would be a lecture about how one of Amy's footballs had made it over the fence or how the cat had pooed in her geraniums again.

"Good morning, Mrs. Jones," she said with as bright a smile as she could manage.

"Oh, I'm sorry Cathryn," she said, "I didn't realise you were poorly."

It dawned on Cathryn how unwell she must look, stood at the door in her slippers, tracksuit bottoms and a low-cut vest top which she had been wearing since the night before. Her curly hair had been calmed into a bun before bed, but now was limply falling to one side.

"Don't worry, Mrs. Jones," Cathryn replied, "How can I help?"

"It's your shed," Mrs. Jones replied, disdain in her voice.

"My shed?" Cathryn said, sleepily wiping her eyes. Of all the things she had expected Mrs. Jones to be complaining about, this wasn't one of them.

"Yes, your shed," Mrs. Jones said, growing frustrated.

"Natalie was working on the foundation this weekend," Cathryn said, "But it's all back in place now."

"That's not the problem," Mrs. Jones said.

"Then, what is?" Cathryn replied, losing patience by the second.

"The *smell*," Mrs. Jones said.

"What smell?" Cathryn asked, hand on hip.

"Go and see," Mrs. Jones said, tutting as she walked back down Cathryn and Natalie's driveway. "You'll see what I mean," she added with raised eyebrows.

Cathryn frowned and closed the front door. *If that damn cat has done something disgusting out there...* she thought. She hadn't wanted to get a cat. It was Natalie who had said it would be good for Amy and Sean to learn how to look after a pet. Whilst Cathryn admitted that the scruffy little kitten they had adopted in 2008 had been very cute, now he was old, grumpy and smelly.

She opened the backdoor and walked up the lawn, past the vegetable patch and to the far end of the garden where the shed was. Mrs. Jones was standing with her neck craning over their shared fence, waiting for Cathryn.

"See?!"

She was triumphant as Cathryn drew closer to the shed and an undeniable odour wafted towards her.

"Ah," Cathryn said. It was faint, but it was unlike anything the cat had ever produced. There was a slight faecal smell mixed in with rotting eggs.

"What are you going to do about it?" Mrs. Jones said.

"It was Mustard, I expect," Cathryn said, "He's old now, he has a gippy tummy sometimes. I'm sure Ted has his accidents too?"

Mrs. Jones wrinkled up her nose at the idea of Ted, her corgi, being anything less than perfect.

"I'll get it cleaned up," Cathryn said, hoping that the conversation would soon be over so she could go back to bed.

"I hope so," Mrs. Jones said, "It's upsetting the dog."

Cathryn nodded with falsified empathy for Ted's plight and headed back inside, hoping she could get a few more hours rest before Sean came back from college.

She lay back on the bed and closed her eyes, attempting to quiet her mind of Mrs. Jones' disapproving voice and thoughts of Sean's journey back on the bus.

Try as she might, worries about being home from work started to flood her mind. After dispelling thoughts of John, she couldn't stop her mind from imagining Mrs. Jones stood at the fence, tutting with a peg on her nose like a cartoon character. The image of Sean sat at the back of the bus with earphones in sprang into her mind. As the bus stopped, another passenger grabbed his phone out of his hand and ran with it out onto the street.

She snapped her eyes open and growled in frustration.

She gave up and headed to the study, hoping that a few hours of work might quiet her mind.

Natalie and Cathryn shared the study, although neither of them worked from home anymore. In the early days of Natalie's marketing company, she had run it from this tiny room, and even now boxes of flyers and business cards were stored under the desk. It had become something of a storage room, with bookcases piled high with stories they didn't have time to read and chest of drawers full of clothes they hoped to one day wear. An exercise bike also stood in one corner, taunting them with an old New Year's resolution to get fit.

Cathryn's laptop was pushed to one side of the desk, and their photo album was out, open at a page with four old photographs on it.

The first was of Natalie and her mother, Bridget. They were sat at a table in La Sosta, a restaurant in Cathryn's hometown of Londonderry that Bridget had always insisted they all go to whenever they visited. Judging from Natalie's camo trousers and bleached hair, it looked like the mid-2000s, just a few years before Bridget passed away. Cathryn shook her head in disbelief as she thought that Sean must have been a toddler, no older than two, when that photo was taken. Natalie looked so different, and yet it felt like yesterday.

The photo underneath that was of Natalie at university in the late 90s, arm around two men that Cathryn didn't recognise. Although they had met at Queen's University, they hadn't started dated until their final year. Natalie had always been very outgoing, keeping an entourage of friends around her, hosting parties in her dorm and organising pub crawls. That was part of the attraction for Cathryn: at 20 she had been far more reserved, and she loved the person she was when she let herself be free, something she had never done until she met Natalie.

The third picture was of the two of them at their wedding in 2001. Cathryn regarded that as their 'real' wedding, but they had legally married once the law changed in 2015. That day had far more significance than the legality of their relationship did. She remembered Natalie's mother's scorn when they told her that they were going to make vows to one another at a friend's café in Drumkeen, the town which would later become their home. Their friend, Grace, had closed the café for the day, hung up string lights, helped them get flowers and made a makeshift arch out of an old trellis. Another friend had taken the photos. They had only a handful of guests, including Cathryn's parents and sister.

Whilst Bridget was always nice to Cathryn, she was "traditional", as she always said, and grappled with Natalie's bisexuality. She didn't view their wedding as legitimate and refused to come. They didn't speak for nearly a year, until Cathryn rang her to tell her that she was pregnant with Sean. The idea of a sperm donor was initially unthinkable to Bridget, but she desperately wanted grandchildren. Their relationship improved after Sean was born and they could all focus on showering him with love.

The final photo was of Bridget holding Sean. She was wearing a sunhat, sat in the back garden at their first house in Letterkenny, just a few miles from where they finally settled. Bridget looked genuinely happy, her face full of love for her grandson. Sean was small, two or three years old, with a Winnie the Pooh t-shirt and blue shorts on. It was a picture that Sean, now 16, found mortifying, but that Natalie and Cathryn knew he would one day cherish as one of very few photos of him with Bridget.

Cathryn wondered why Natalie had been looking through the photo album that morning. She presumed she had been thinking about her mother, as she often did. Cathryn made a mental note to get the picture of Bridget and Sean blown up and framed for Natalie's next birthday. Whilst Sean might be livid at her for it, Natalie would be thrilled.

She put the album back on the shelf above the desk and sat down to work.

Cathryn awoke to the tell-tale sound of the front door slamming – Sean was home. She had fallen asleep, head on hands, hands on the keyboard, her spreadsheet still open.

"Hi, love," she called out, her voice croaking with a yawn.

"Mum?" Sean replied. She listened to his heavy footfall as he came up the stairs to find her in the study. He appeared in the doorway and said, "Why are you home?"

"Just a bit poorly, love," she said, "How was college?"

"Boring," Sean said, walking to his room. She heard him throw his backpack down, "I'm sleeping over Harry's tonight. Getting the bus at seven-ish," he added.

"Are you now?" Cathryn said, a little bemused at the way he had asserted it rather than asked, "Make sure you're back in time for college tomorrow."

"No classes 'til lunchtime," Sean replied, "Don't stress, Mum," he added as he closed his bedroom door.

Cathryn sighed. Don't stress. Good advice from her quickly maturing boy. She closed the laptop and headed down to the kitchen as she realised that she hadn't eaten all day. It wasn't unusual – she was just too busy to think about food most workdays. She put together a sandwich and headed back to the study to continue with the spreadsheet.

Sean was still in his room. He was laughing raucously, but she couldn't make out what he was saying. He must have been speaking to his friends on Discord.

A few hours later at nearly 6pm, the door slammed again. Cathryn smiled to herself – Sean had clearly picked up that habit from Natalie.

"Your favourite mother is home!" Natalie joked, walking from room to room downstairs before heading up the stairs.

"How was work?" Cathryn asked, swivelling the desk chair to face Natalie as she walked in.

"Lousy," Natalie said, chewing a Kit Kat half-heartedly, "Did you stay home today? Your bag is still in the living room."

"Yeah, was just feeling a bit rough."

"Yeah, you look it," Natalie said affectionately, running a

hand over Cathryn's lop-sided bun, "You're working too hard."

"Probably," Cathryn admitted. She didn't mention the lack of sleep. She didn't want to ruin the moment by sparking judgemental comments from Natalie.

"I got you a present," Natalie said with a smile.

She pulled a pack of Wine Gums from the pocket of her blazer and tossed them playfully onto the desk.

"Christ, it's been years since I had these," Cathryn said. She had blasted through bag after bag of them at university and had at one point sworn off of them completely. She was hit with a strange nostalgia and sense of guilt as she opened the pack and breathed in the artificial fruit smell, "Did you go to the shops?"

"Just the Supervalu in Donegal. Only a euro - don't I spoil you?"

"Donegal?"

"I had to drive there for a client meeting. Some coffee shop. Bloody awful croissants," Natalie said, reaching over and taking a Wine Gum.

"Hey, you said those were a present," Cathryn teased.

"Yeah, yeah," Natalie said, "What's for dinner?"

"You're all business tonight, aren't you?"

"Long day," Natalie said, and then added under her breath, "Long year."

"I know that feeling," Cathryn said, standing up to kiss her on the cheek, "Takeaway?"

"Sounds grand."

Sean left for his friend's house before the pizza arrived, leaving Natalie and Cathryn alone for the first time in months.

They settled down in the living room with their pizza.

"Netflix?" Natalie said, manoeuvring the remote to try and get it to work.

"Perfect," Cathryn said, tucking into a slice as the house phone rang. She answered it, placing it under her cheek and shoulder as she continued to load the takeaway onto her plate.

"Hi Mum," the tiny voice came.

"Hi sweetie, how's camp?" Cathryn looked at Natalie as she spoke to signal that it was Amy on the phone and to wait to start the programme.

"It's amazing, we went abseiling this morning!" Amy replied, voice lit up with excitement.

"Oh wow," Cathryn said, only half-listening as Amy continued with her list of activities. It was her first school trip of secondary school. It had been nerve-wracking for both Amy and her mothers to entertain the idea of her going away for two weeks without them. Whilst they had had time to adjust to the idea of Sean being a teenager, they still thought of Amy as a little child, but she was quickly growing up.

"Let me say hi!" Natalie whispered, reaching out for the phone.

"Okay, okay, Mum wants to speak to you," Cathryn said, handing the phone over to Natalie and continuing with her pizza.

"Sounds amazing!" Natalie said. She was much better at faking genuine enthusiasm than Cathryn

Unless she didn't need to fake it, Cathryn thought.

After a few minutes of questions and answers, Natalie said, "Can't wait to see you soon sweetie. Night now!"

Natalie hung up the phone, putting it on the couch cushion and sighing, "She's growing up too quick."

"I know," Cathryn said, "It seems like only yesterday that

Sean was a baby, let alone Amy. That reminds me – I saw those pictures you had out."

"Pictures?" Natalie said, eyes on the episode of *Jessica Jones* that she had put on.

"The photo album," Cathryn said.

"Oh," Natalie said, looking at her. She looked almost surprised for a moment and Cathryn met her eyes with confusion, "Yes, I was just looking through," Natalie added after a few seconds, returning to her pizza.

"Yeah, I saw," Cathryn said, marking her weird expression, "There was a lovely one of Sean and your mum."

"Oh, yeah, there was," Natalie said absent-mindedly, "In La Sosta, right?"

"No, the one with Sean was at our place – at Kemp Road."

"Oh, yes that's right, Kemp Road," Natalie corrected herself. She only sounded half-sure of her words.

"Our old place in Letterkenny," Cathryn added, watching Natalie nodding along.

"That's right," Natalie said, "I like that photo."

"Me too," Cathryn said, deciding to drop it.

"Did you do anything today?" Natalie said, muffled as she tugged with her teeth on a rope of cheese that was pulling away from her pizza.

"Just vegged out," Cathryn said, "Although, Mrs. Nosey came round."

"What now? Amy's ball?" Natalie said with a chuckle, chewing her bite loudly.

"That's what I thought, but no," Cathryn said, finishing a slice and leaning forward to grab another from the coffee table.

"Then what?"

"She was complaining about the shed," Cathryn said, sitting back with her slice. Pizza sauce dripped onto her shirt and she swore, scrubbing at it with a bit of tissue. When she looked back up, she realised Natalie hadn't replied. She had stopped chewing and was staring intently at Cathryn, "What?" Cathryn said.

"What about the shed?" Natalie said, her voice uncharacteristically stern.

"What?"

"The fucking shed. What did she say about it, Cathryn?"

"Jesus," Cathryn said, putting her slice down, "What's with you? She was moaning about a smell. Probably Mustard."

Natalie didn't reply. Her eyes blinked rapidly, flitting from one side of Cathryn's face to the other. Cathryn stared back with one eyebrow raised, waiting for the punchline.

Natalie looked down, and her face changed back to normal. She said, "Yeah, probably the cat. I'll go out and see if I can find the mess later."

"Okay..." Cathryn replied, still not sure why Natalie had reacted so dramatically.

They carried on watching the TV in silence and finished the pizza.

Cathryn headed to bed first, knowing full well she wouldn't sleep, but she enjoyed the routine of sitting up in bed and watching TV. It made her feel hope each night that she might doze off during one of the programmes.

She never did.

Natalie usually came to bed at 11pm, read her book for half an hour and then begged Cathryn to keep the TV volume low so she could sleep.

11pm came, but Natalie did not.

Midnight, still no Natalie.

Cathryn pulled her slippers back on and walked down the stairs, expecting to find Natalie in the living room, asleep on the sofa.

She wasn't there.

Cathryn headed to the kitchen and grabbed a glass of

water. The cat circled her legs, hoping for some food, although Cathryn knew Natalie had fed him when she got home from work.

"Shoo," she said, stepping over him and heading to the kitchen table to sit down.

As she did, she could hear a rhythmic thumping. It wasn't loud, but it was constant. She looked around the kitchen in search of the noise. She wondered if Natalie was in the downstairs bathroom, and a flash of anxiety ran through her as she imagined her drowning in the tub, banging on the side for help.

She sprang up and ran to the bathroom, pushing open the door.

The bathroom was empty. The noise was fainter at this end of the house.

She walked back over to the kitchen table and listened.

She realised it was coming from the garden.

It was raining now; a steady, sad trickle that could soak you in minutes. She pulled on the wellies she kept by the backdoor and took an umbrella from the coat rack.

"Nat?" she called into the darkness.

She traipsed over the lawn as the noise grew clearer. She ducked past the runner beans in the vegetable patch and kept going to the farthest end of the garden.

A sinking feeling grew in her as she realised where the noise was coming from: the shed at the top of the garden.

She rounded the corner of the vegetable patch, the stone path coming to its end at another patch of grass.

Cathryn let the umbrella fall from her hand. The shed was down, the planks in bits on the floor and Natalie was digging into the foundation with a shovel.

"Nat!" Cathryn called over the rain, "What the fuck?"

Natalie turned around, surprise and guilt colouring her face in equal measure. Her bob was stuck to her ears and neck with the driving rain and there were brown and black smudges all over her cheeks and forehead. Her blazer was on the grass, sodden and crumpled, and her pastel pink jumpsuit was clinging to her figure so tightly that it was almost see through. She looked vulnerable, a state Cathryn rarely saw her in.

They looked at each other for a few drawn out moments.

"What's going on? And don't lie to me," Cathryn finally said, her voice steadier than she felt.

"Okay," Natalie said, pushing up on the shovel and climbing out of the dip she had dug, "But I don't know where to start."

She sounded strange. Cathryn could see tears in Natalie's eyes. It hadn't been immediately obvious as the rain had been washing down her face, but Cathryn could hear it in her voice and see the puffiness in her eyes.

She had only seen Natalie cry a handful of times in their relationship. The first time had been their wedding day. The second was the day her mum died. Both of the children's births. And finally, at their friend Grace's funeral.

Fear flooded her senses, "Just tell me what you're doing."

Cathryn noticed the smell was stronger despite the rain. It was still subtle, but the putridity was enough to make her want to cover her nose.

"Just look," Natalie said, barely getting the words out among sobs.

Cathryn walked forward, leaning over to look into the foundation of the shed.

Natalie had been filling the foundation in the previous weekend, Cathryn presumed with concrete, but as she looked in, she only saw mud and gravel.

She looked at Natalie in puzzlement. Natalie's eyes were wide with horror and Cathryn looked again.

Among the mud and growing puddles of water was a shape. It was long, two metres or so.

As her eyes pieced together the scene, she saw it something wrapped in blue tarpaulin.

Her eyes drifted over the shape and Natalie's horror become her own.

It was a human shape. A body.

"Oh god, oh god," Cathryn said.

"Don't scream," Natalie said, her voice begging rather than commanding. She was sniffling violently.

"What is going on?" Cathryn whispered frantically. It was all she could bring herself to say.

She couldn't keep hold of any form of her reality. She had wanted to keep grounded, to stay present in her mind as she understood what was happening, even though there was a big part of her consciousness that was trying to float away, to get away from the shock and terror that was shooting through every nerve in her chest.

It became apparent that Natalie couldn't reply at all. Her mouth was opening, but nothing was coming out. Cathryn was so used to her being the strong one. She gathered herself together.

"What the fuck did you do?"

"I didn't mean to," Natalie said eventually, "I didn't want to."

Cathryn's soul sank back into her as the certainty of the reply hit her.

"What...?" Cathryn couldn't finish the words.

Natalie stood up and came towards her. Cathryn took a step back, hands out in front of her.

Natalie breathed in deeply and steadied her sobs. She said, "He came round on Saturday when you and the kids went round your mum's. I didn't mean to. He came at me. I..."

She stopped and wiped her face on the sleeve of her jumpsuit.

Cathryn saw Natalie in a new light, as if she was meeting her for the first time. She fruitlessly cast her mind back, wanting to return to a time when she didn't know that her wife was a killer.

"Who?" Cathryn said.

"An ex."

"*Who?*" Cathryn said again, anger edging out the fear. The anger felt unreasonable when she looked at Natalie's distraught face, but she couldn't shake her fury. Fury that their life would change. Fury at her wife's mistake.

"His name was Rob," she said, the name falling from her tongue like a declaration of love.

"Rob?" Cathryn repeated. She didn't know the name.

"We messed around at uni for a few months. First year. Nothing serious, just sex. Companionship. Just someone to be with," Natalie said.

"Why was he here?"

"I don't know," Natalie said, "He found our address on the business' website, it's still listed on there."

"Why was he here?" Cathryn said again, shaking her head in disbelief, "Why?" she spat out, anger consuming her.

"I don't know!" Natalie said desperately, "He still held a torch for me, I think. I told him I was busy. I was fixing the shed. I offered him a cuppa. We talked while I worked."

"Why was he here?" Cathryn repeated.

"Alright," Natalie said, "He found out something."

"What?" Cathryn said.

"I was pregnant once," Natalie said slowly, "I didn't tell him, because what we had... it wasn't anything serious. It was just a fling. And I really didn't want... that... child, I mean... not yet."

"He was fuming," Cathryn said.

"Yeah," Natalie said, "He found out from a mutual friend of ours from back then -Joe. Joe was the one who took me to get it sorted."

"The pregnancy?" Cathryn asked.

"Yes, the pregnancy," Natalie said. "Apparently Rob met up with Joe on Friday. They're still friends – were still friends. They reminisced, got drunk. Truthfully, it sounds like they were shit-faced. Joe let it slip, that fucker."

"And then what? Rob came here the next day?"

"Yeah. And he just got angrier and angrier the more I explained it," Natalie started to cry fresh tears, "He came at me, he was shouting, calling me a whore, a traitor, a baby killer," Natalie drew in her breath and added clearly, "Then he said I didn't deserve to be a mother."

Cathryn's mind clicked. It was a sore spot.

She cast her mind back to the phone call she had made to Bridget all those years ago. Natalie had been listening in on the other receiver, anxiously waiting for her mother's approval or rejection, even though it was after the fact.

Sean had already been created.

"How?" Bridget had said.

"A sperm donor," Cathryn had replied, "A friend of a friend was willing to do it. He gave us his medical history, a clean bill of health. No family conditions. He's sporty, clever, a good guy."

"Right," Bridget had said, "So the child... isn't Natalie's at all."

"Well, not biologically," Cathryn had said, heart racing as she knew Natalie could hear the conversation, "But we're both the child's parents."

"It's not right," Bridget had said, and Cathryn's hope fell, "She doesn't deserve to call herself a mother."

Of course, Natalie had known it wasn't true. She knew they would love their children. And when Bridget attended the birth, everything changed. Her love for Sean overrode every thought she had about his parentage, but Cathryn knew Natalie had never forgiven her for her words.

And now Cathryn heard Natalie repeat her mother's words, stood in their garden in the rain, face contorted with the pain of sixteen years ago.

Cathryn walked across and hugged her. At first Natalie didn't hug her back, her arms falling limply at her side, but after a few moments, she gripped her back, crying into her neck.

"How did you... do it?" Cathryn whispered.

"I was holding the shovel. I didn't think. I just swung it at him."

"And he definitely... died?" Cathryn wrapped her lips around the word they hadn't spoken yet.

"Yes," Natalie said, "I checked."

"Blood?" Cathryn said, looking at the grass.

"No," Natalie said, "No blood."

They stood holding each other for a few minutes more before Cathryn said, "We have to move him."

"I know," Natalie said.

"Did anyone see? Oh god," Cathryn asked, "The Joneses?"

"No," Natalie said, "They took their caravan somewhere for the weekend."

"That's something at least."

"Yes," Natalie replied robotically, the enormity of their conversation bearing down on both of them.

"Did Joe know he was coming to see you?" Cathryn asked Natalie.

"I don't know," Natalie admitted.

"Joe hasn't called his phone?" Cathryn said.

"Wasn't one on him," Natalie said, "I checked."

"Car?"

"Bus," Natalie said, "He complained about it."

"Wife, girlfriend?"

"Not that he mentioned," Natalie said, "Nothing on his Facebook either."

"You looked at his Facebook?"

"I..." Natalie shook her head in guilt, "Yes. Yes, I did."

"Then we can get on with this," Cathryn said, "And just hope he didn't have anyone to tell that he was coming here."

"Oh god," Natalie sighed, leaning against the handle of the shovel.

Cathryn felt calm. Calmer than she ever would have predicted that she would be in a situation like this. The shock had numbed her, leaving room for nothing but sharp pragmatism. She had always been the sensible to Natalie's impulsivity and that might just be their salvation.

"I don't know what to do," Natalie said, still no emotion in her voice, "What should we do?"

There was worry on Natalie's face, but it dawned on Cathryn that it wasn't over Rob. Natalie had been waiting for Cathryn to turn, walk away, leave her to her fate. Cathryn thought for a moment. She thought she should be afraid of Natalie and reject her for the crime she had committed. But only one feeling rose to the surface.

"We're not going to let this ruin the life we've built," Cathryn said with certainty, "To affect everything we've done to get to this day. This lovely house. Our beautiful kids. Our marriage."

At the final word, Natalie looked up and met Cathryn's eyes, relief overtaking her at the confirmation from Cathryn. It hadn't seemed to occur to her that the marriage was salvageable, that Cathryn would be willing to look past this.

"Thank you," Natalie said, her emotions creeping back into her tone, making her voice wobble, "Thank you," she repeated breathlessly.

"We have to get him out of here," Cathryn said quietly, "Somewhere remote. Somewhere no one will look."

"The beach," Natalie said without hesitation. Cathryn knew with a crushing feeling where she meant.

"The beach at Rinmore Point," Cathryn said quietly. The place where Natalie had proposed to her. The place they took the kids every summer. Where they scattered her dad's ashes.

"Len's kayak is still strapped to the top of my car," Natalie said. Len was one of her employee's. They had taken the kayak on a work weekend away a few weeks before, putting it on Natalie's 4X4 because it had a roof rack.

"We have to go, now," Cathryn said.

It was a long process to move the body out of the back gate and along the alleyway next to their house, into the back seat of the car. He was heavy, and the odour was nauseating beyond anything Cathryn had ever experienced.

Cathryn packed bleach and sponges, and they discussed how best to burn their clothes when they returned. The Joneses seemed to be asleep, their house in total darkness as Natalie pulled out of the driveway.

It was over an hour's drive, rain lashing against the windscreen the entire way, but they knew the journey well and muscle memory moved them forward. The smell was unbearable even with the windows open - a constant reminder of their task.

The familiar sight of fields dotted with sheep and an expanse of sea was visible, but barely, when they arrived in the early hours of the morning. There were very few houses on the stretch of road, and they were confident they wouldn't be disturbed.

They pulled the kayak out before loading the body into it, hoping that in the rare instance of an onlooker, they would merely be surprised at the midnight boat trip rather than spotting the corpse.

Mercifully, the kayak had wheels to pull it along and their trip down onto the stone shore was made somewhat more bearable.

"What now?" Natalie said.

Cathryn was dumbstruck for a moment, the sweetness of all the memories colliding with the dark reality they were facing.

"We put rocks in the tarp," Cathryn said, "And swim out with the boat. Once we're out there, it's a case of tipping it over, bringing it back and leaving as quickly as we can."

They worked silently to collect rocks and place them in the first fold of the tarp. Natalie sliced the inside of her hand picking up a piece of slate. Cathryn grabbed her hand as she was about to put it in.

"Not this one – blood, Nat," Cathryn said.

"Oh shit," Natalie said. Cathryn pulled off a sock and bound it around Natalie's hand.

"Don't use that one, okay?" she said.

It took an hour to finish the task back out of the water on a different bit of beach to where they had gone in. The low tide had created a sandy crevice and they had to get the kayak across it. Cathryn climbed through the ditch with it first, reaching out to accept the front of the kayak and heaved it over to the other side. Turning back to the ditch, she reached out a hand to help Natalie out of it.

Their hands clasped, the mud of Cathryn's mixing with the blood on Natalie's.

"We can't ever talk about this," Natalie said.

"I promise," Cathryn whispered.

They continued up the shoreline back towards the car, being careful to stick to the waves. Sea spray clung to their hair, making it both sticky and crispy with salt.

The water raked over their path and it was almost as if they had never been there. Cathryn knew they'd never be able to come back.

No more picnics.

No more sandcastles.

All memories washed away with their guilt.

They walked back to the car and secured the kayak. Sitting in the front seats, they gripped each other's hands and Cathryn sighed.

"Back home," she said.

"Yeah," Natalie said. "Home."

Coming in 2021

Ship in Distress

T. C. Emerys

A Collection of Short Fiction

ABOUT THE AUTHOR

T. C. Emerys is the pen name of writer and ghostwriter Tegan Baker. Born in England, Baker studied for her B.A in English Literature, an M.A in Medieval Studies and an MPhil in Medieval Literature.

In her spare time, Baker is an avid equestrian, pianist and book lover.

Follow her on Instagram @tcemerys.writer

ABOUT "THE WEIGHT OF RAIN"

Is there anything more British than rain? Not pretty deluges of it that couples kiss under in rom-coms, but grey, sludgy, cold, joy-sapping rain.

Perhaps unusually, the first story to take shape in this collection was the titular one: *The Weight of Rain*.

The story came to me, without any intention of developing it into something more, as two pages of simple prose about a woman mourning the loss of her mentor. In some ways, the inspiration for this feeling came from the loss of my own literary mentor a few years earlier, a woman some six decades older than me, whose loss made a considerable impact on me personally and as a writer.

Whilst Henna and Cora in *The Weight of Rain* and *Henna* don't wholly resemble myself and my mentor, the relationship of women helping other women was one that I felt the need to explore within the two stories given my own considerable helping hand into the world of literature.

The theme of rain was one that developed later, when I realised what all Britons truly know from birth: that rain defines our grey little isles. It is a love/hate relationship. It's a terrible cliché that the British are obsessed with talking about the weather, and I suppose I haven't helped that image with this book, but nevertheless rain became my theme and Britain and Ireland became my settings.

I wanted a taste of each of our nations to be in the stories, but it is only from the diligent help of many talented readers across the UK and Ireland that I was able to.

I wish for these stories to give you comfort for your losses and hope as you stand under gloomy rain-filled skies, wherever you are in the world.

ACKNOWLEDGMENTS

Besides the thanks that go to my wonderful family and friends who supported me whilst writing this, I would also like to thank a few special individuals without whom *The Weight of Rain* would have been completely lost.

My sincerest thanks to my wonderful editor Annelie Widholm for not just wading through my writing but also for her useful insights and necessary critiques. A writer is nothing without a good editor and I'm very glad to have found such a supportive one.

My further thanks to Rhiannon, better known as the exceptionally talented LunarBirdArt, for the art included in the chapter breaks. They add so much to the book and I am so appreciative of the time you spent on them.

My additional thanks to the many people who beta read some or all of the stories. Your time, comments and patience were gratefully received.

My gratitude also goes to the wonderful people across social media, especially The Gumption Club, who offered support, complimented the extracts and joined in with the launch. Social media is not always known for its supportive environment, but I can say that the self-publishing community are bolstering and critical in perfect proportion. Thank you for your candour.

Finally, all my thanks and love to Jason. For everything.

NOTES

Undeveloped History was first published on *Reedsy Prompts* as an entry into their 51st Short Story Competition on 24th July 2020. The given prompt for this submission was "Write a story about someone who returns as an adult to a place they last visited as a child".

You can read this story on *Reedsy Prompts* by visiting the following link:

https://blog.reedsy.com/creative-writing-prompts/contests/51/submissions/26629/